DISNEY

DESCENDANTS

FRIGHT AT THE MUSEUM

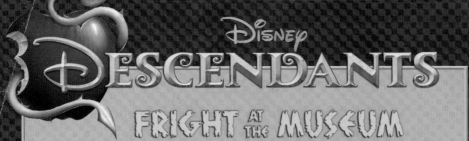

Disney

DESCENDANTS

FRIGHT AT THE MUSEUM

STORY BY
DELILAH S. DAWSON

PENCILS BY
ANNA CATTISH

INKS BY
ELIZAVETA SHOKAREVA

COLORS BY
ANNA CATTISH
WITH ASSISTANCE FROM
DARIA NIKITINA & ELIZAVETA KUZNETSOVA

LETTERS BY
CHRISTA MIESNER

DESIGN BY
CHRISTA MIESNER & SAM MURRAY

EDITORIAL ASSISTANT
ANNI PERHEENTUPA

EDITS BY
ELIZABETH BREI

GROUP EDITOR
DENTON J. TIPTON

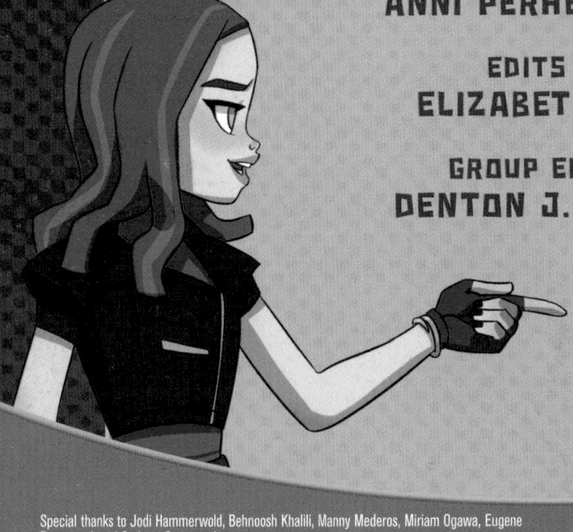

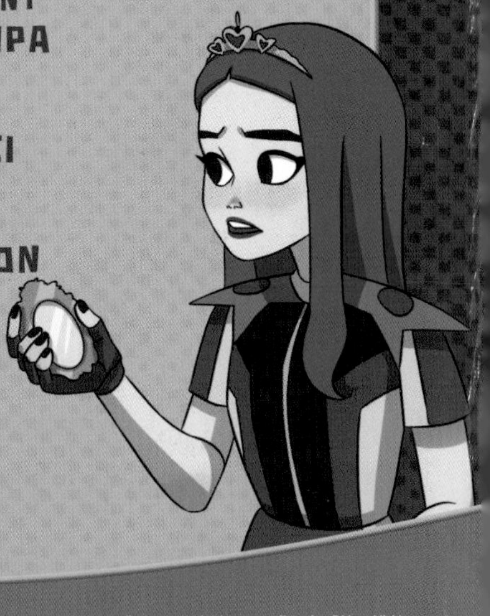

Special thanks to Jodi Hammerwold, Behnoosh Khalili, Manny Mederos, Miriam Ogawa, Eugene Paraszczuk and Carlotta Quattrocolo.

For international rights, contact licensing@idwpublishing.com

ISBN: 978-1-68405-415-2

23 22 21 20 1 2 3 4

IDW®
www.IDWPUBLISHING.com

Chris Ryall, President & Publisher/CCO • **Cara Morrison**, Chief Financial Officer • **Matthew Ruzicka**, Chief Accounting Officer • **David Hedgecock**, Associate Publisher • **John Barber**, Editor-in-Chief • **Justin Eisinger**, Editorial Director, Graphic Novels and Collections • **Jerry Bennington**, VP of New Product Development • **Lorelei Bunjes**, VP of Technology & Information Services • **Jud Meyers**, Sales Director • **Anna Morrow**, Marketing Director • **Tara McCrillis**, Director of Design & Production • **Mike Ford**, Director of Operations • **Rebekah Cahalin**, General Manager

Ted Adams and Robbie Robbins, IDW Founders

Facebook: facebook.com/idwpublishing • Twitter: @idwpublishing • YouTube: youtube.com/idwpublishing
Tumblr: tumblr.idwpublishing.com • Instagram: instagram.com/idwpublishing

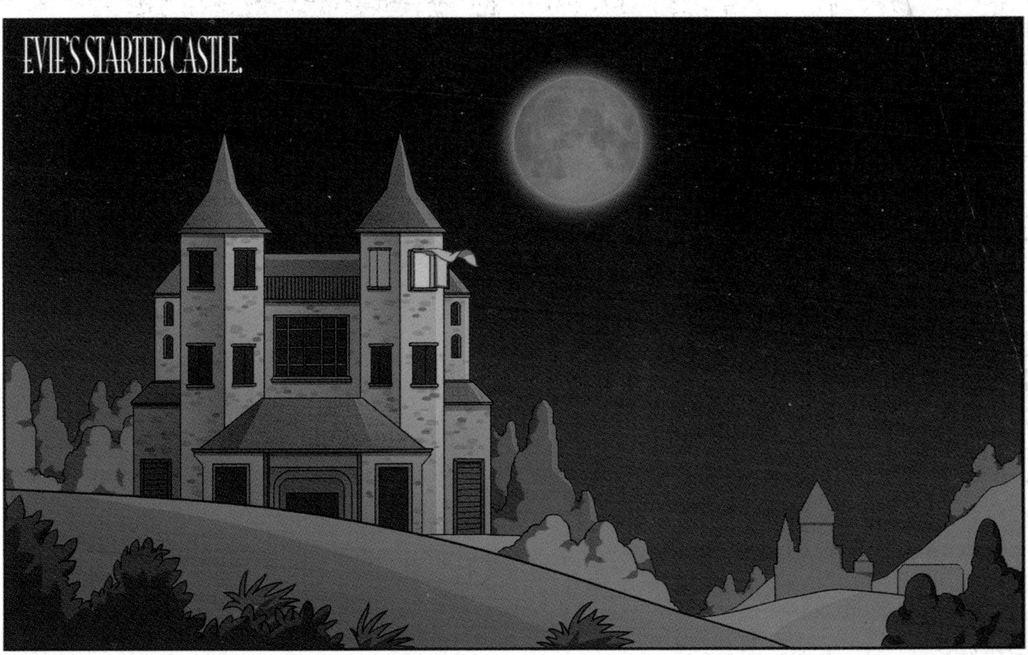
EVIE'S STARTER CASTLE.

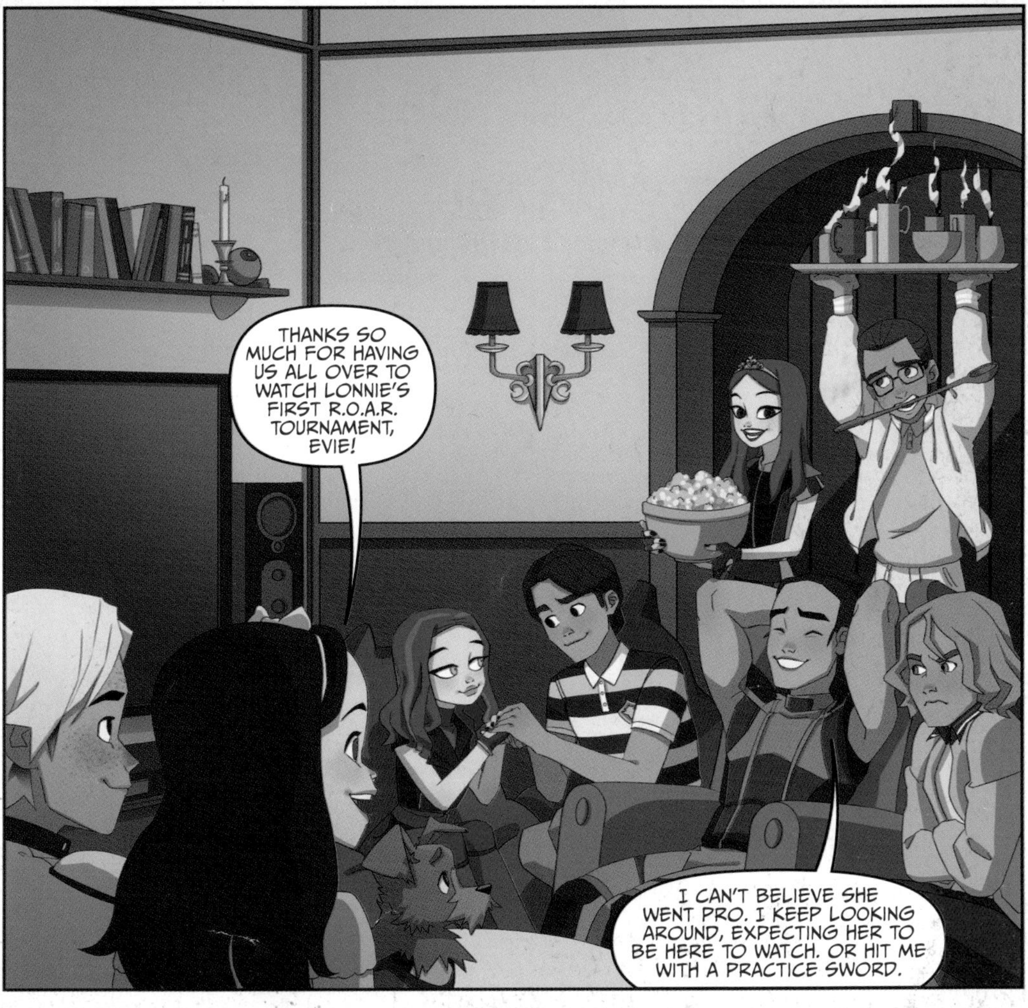
THANKS SO MUCH FOR HAVING US ALL OVER TO WATCH LONNIE'S FIRST R.O.A.R. TOURNAMENT, EVIE!
I CAN'T BELIEVE SHE WENT PRO. I KEEP LOOKING AROUND, EXPECTING HER TO BE HERE TO WATCH. OR HIT ME WITH A PRACTICE SWORD.

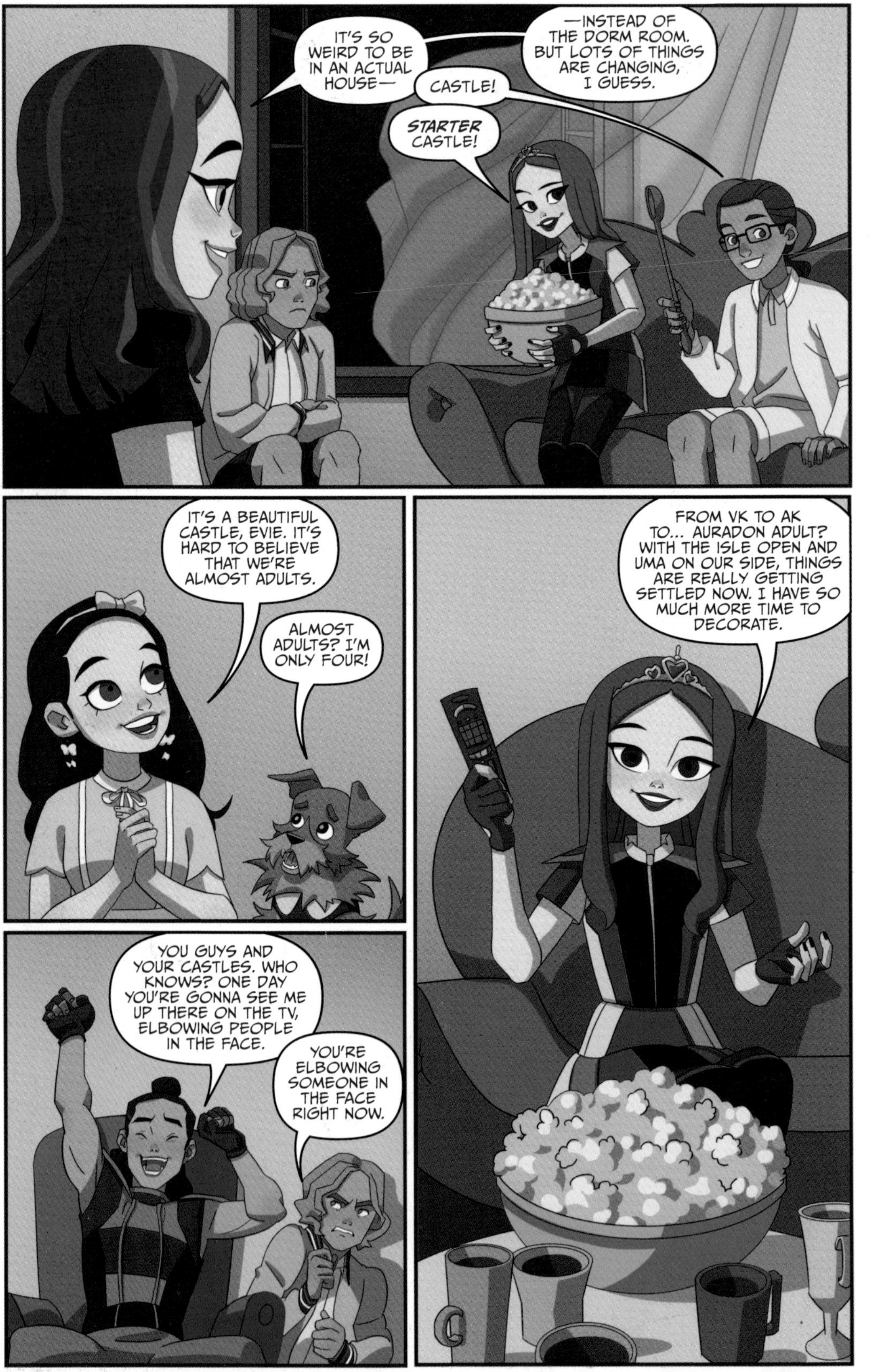
IT'S SO WEIRD TO BE IN AN ACTUAL HOUSE—
CASTLE!
STARTER CASTLE!
—INSTEAD OF THE DORM ROOM. BUT LOTS OF THINGS ARE CHANGING, I GUESS.
IT'S A BEAUTIFUL CASTLE, EVIE. IT'S HARD TO BELIEVE THAT WE'RE ALMOST ADULTS.
ALMOST ADULTS? I'M ONLY FOUR!
FROM VK TO AK TO... AURADON ADULT? WITH THE ISLE OPEN AND UMA ON OUR SIDE, THINGS ARE REALLY GETTING SETTLED NOW. I HAVE SO MUCH MORE TIME TO DECORATE.
YOU GUYS AND YOUR CASTLES. WHO KNOWS? ONE DAY YOU'RE GONNA SEE ME UP THERE ON THE TV, ELBOWING PEOPLE IN THE FACE.
YOU'RE ELBOWING SOMEONE IN THE FACE RIGHT NOW.

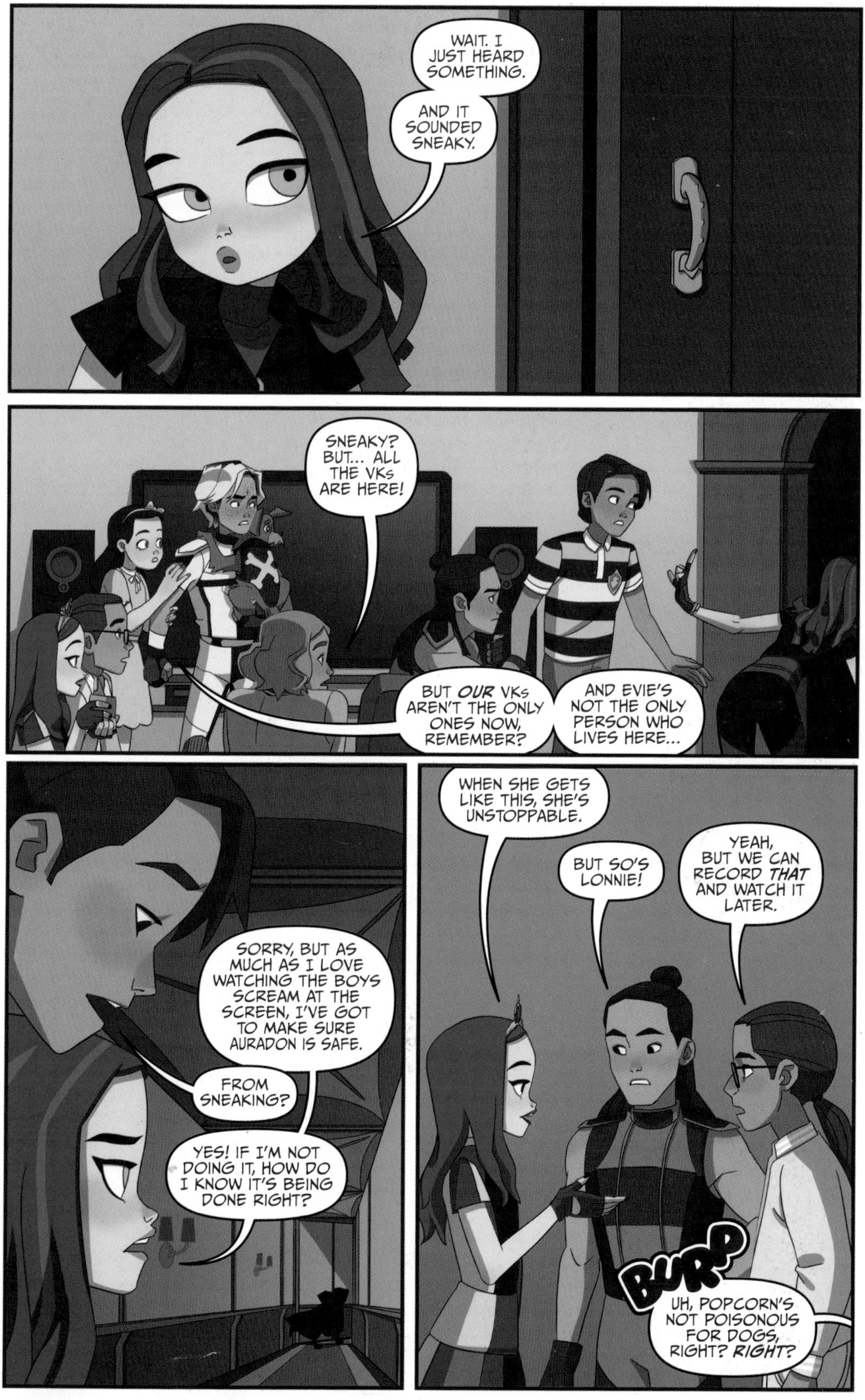
WAIT. I JUST HEARD SOMETHING.
AND IT SOUNDED SNEAKY.
SNEAKY? BUT... ALL THE VKs ARE HERE!
BUT OUR VKs AREN'T THE ONLY ONES NOW, REMEMBER?
AND EVIE'S NOT THE ONLY PERSON WHO LIVES HERE...
SORRY, BUT AS MUCH AS I LOVE WATCHING THE BOYS SCREAM AT THE SCREEN, I'VE GOT TO MAKE SURE AURADON IS SAFE.
FROM SNEAKING?
YES! IF I'M NOT DOING IT, HOW DO I KNOW IT'S BEING DONE RIGHT?
WHEN SHE GETS LIKE THIS, SHE'S UNSTOPPABLE.
BUT SO'S LONNIE!
YEAH, BUT WE CAN RECORD THAT AND WATCH IT LATER.
BURP
UH, POPCORN'S NOT POISONOUS FOR DOGS, RIGHT? RIGHT?

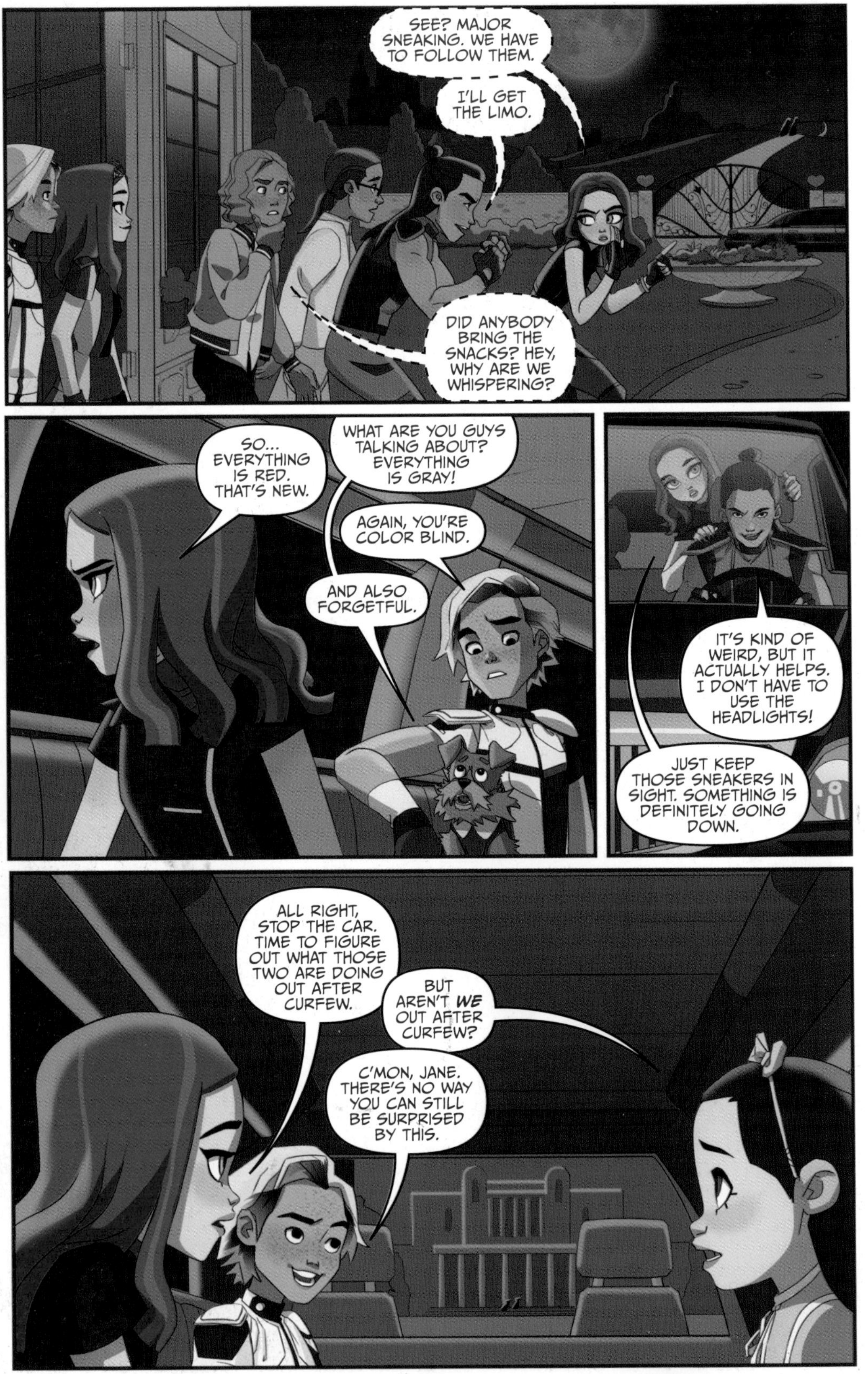

SEE? MAJOR SNEAKING. WE HAVE TO FOLLOW THEM.
I'LL GET THE LIMO.
DID ANYBODY BRING THE SNACKS? HEY, WHY ARE WE WHISPERING?
SO... EVERYTHING IS RED. THAT'S NEW.
WHAT ARE YOU GUYS TALKING ABOUT? EVERYTHING IS GRAY!
AGAIN, YOU'RE COLOR BLIND.
AND ALSO FORGETFUL.
IT'S KIND OF WEIRD, BUT IT ACTUALLY HELPS. I DON'T HAVE TO USE THE HEADLIGHTS!
JUST KEEP THOSE SNEAKERS IN SIGHT. SOMETHING IS DEFINITELY GOING DOWN.
ALL RIGHT, STOP THE CAR. TIME TO FIGURE OUT WHAT THOSE TWO ARE DOING OUT AFTER CURFEW.
BUT AREN'T **WE** OUT AFTER CURFEW?
C'MON, JANE. THERE'S NO WAY YOU CAN STILL BE SURPRISED BY THIS.

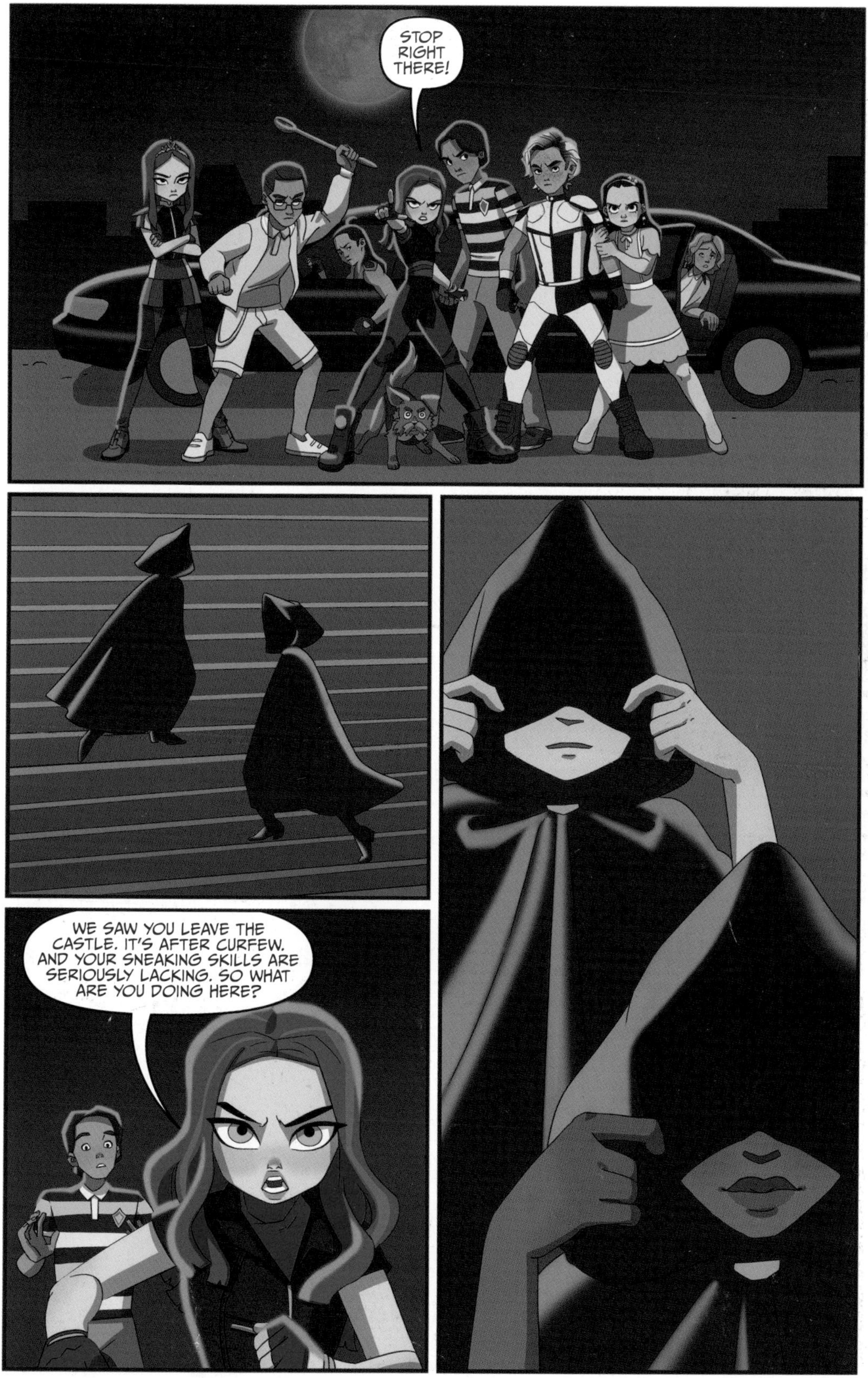
STOP RIGHT THERE!
WE SAW YOU LEAVE THE CASTLE. IT'S AFTER CURFEW. AND YOUR SNEAKING SKILLS ARE SERIOUSLY LACKING. SO WHAT ARE YOU DOING HERE?

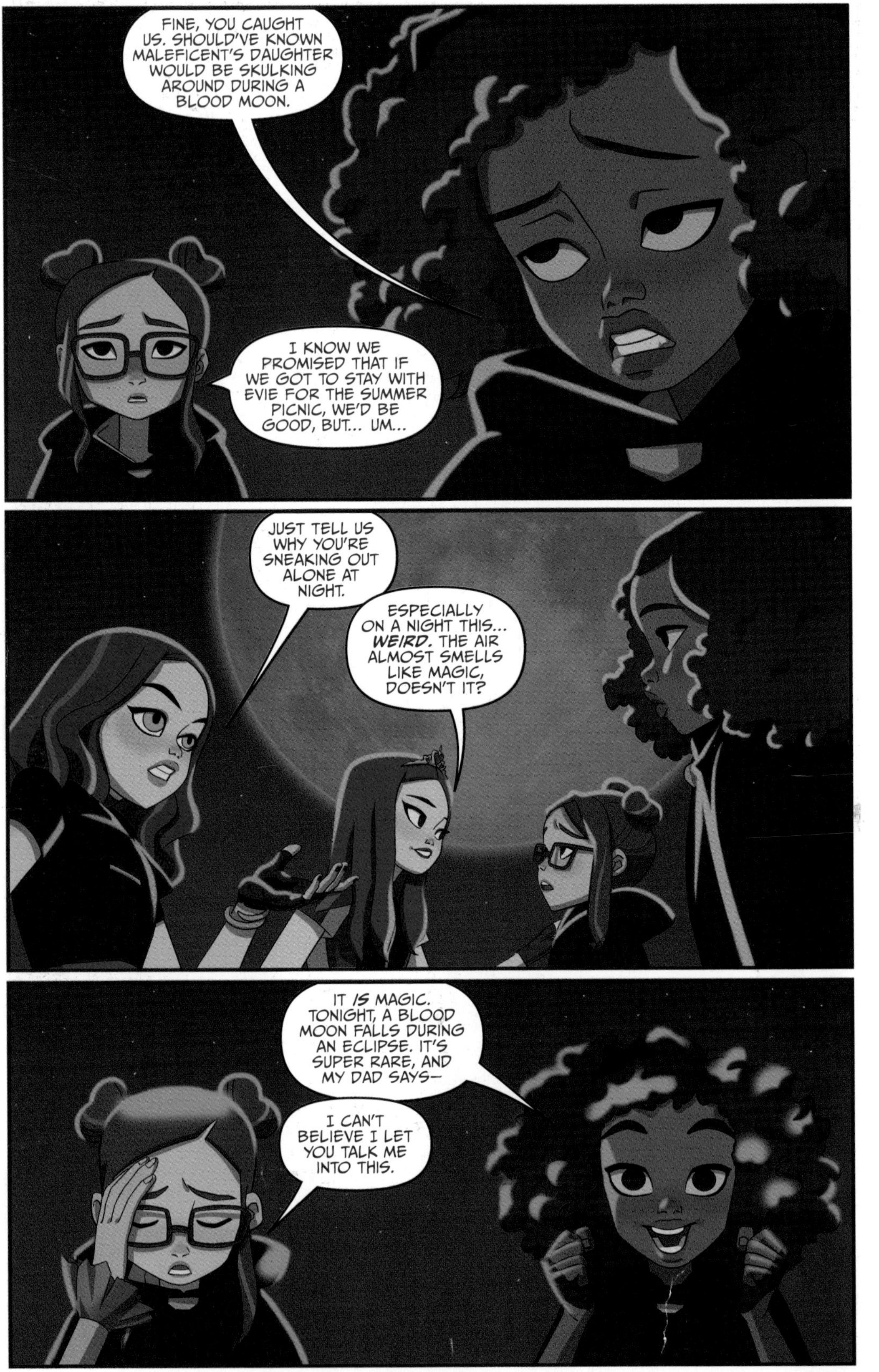
FINE, YOU CAUGHT US. SHOULD'VE KNOWN MALEFICENT'S DAUGHTER WOULD BE SKULKING AROUND DURING A BLOOD MOON.
I KNOW WE PROMISED THAT IF WE GOT TO STAY WITH EVIE FOR THE SUMMER PICNIC, WE'D BE GOOD, BUT... UM...
JUST TELL US WHY YOU'RE SNEAKING OUT ALONE AT NIGHT.
ESPECIALLY ON A NIGHT THIS... WEIRD. THE AIR ALMOST SMELLS LIKE MAGIC, DOESN'T IT?
IT IS MAGIC. TONIGHT, A BLOOD MOON FALLS DURING AN ECLIPSE. IT'S SUPER RARE, AND MY DAD SAYS—
I CAN'T BELIEVE I LET YOU TALK ME INTO THIS.

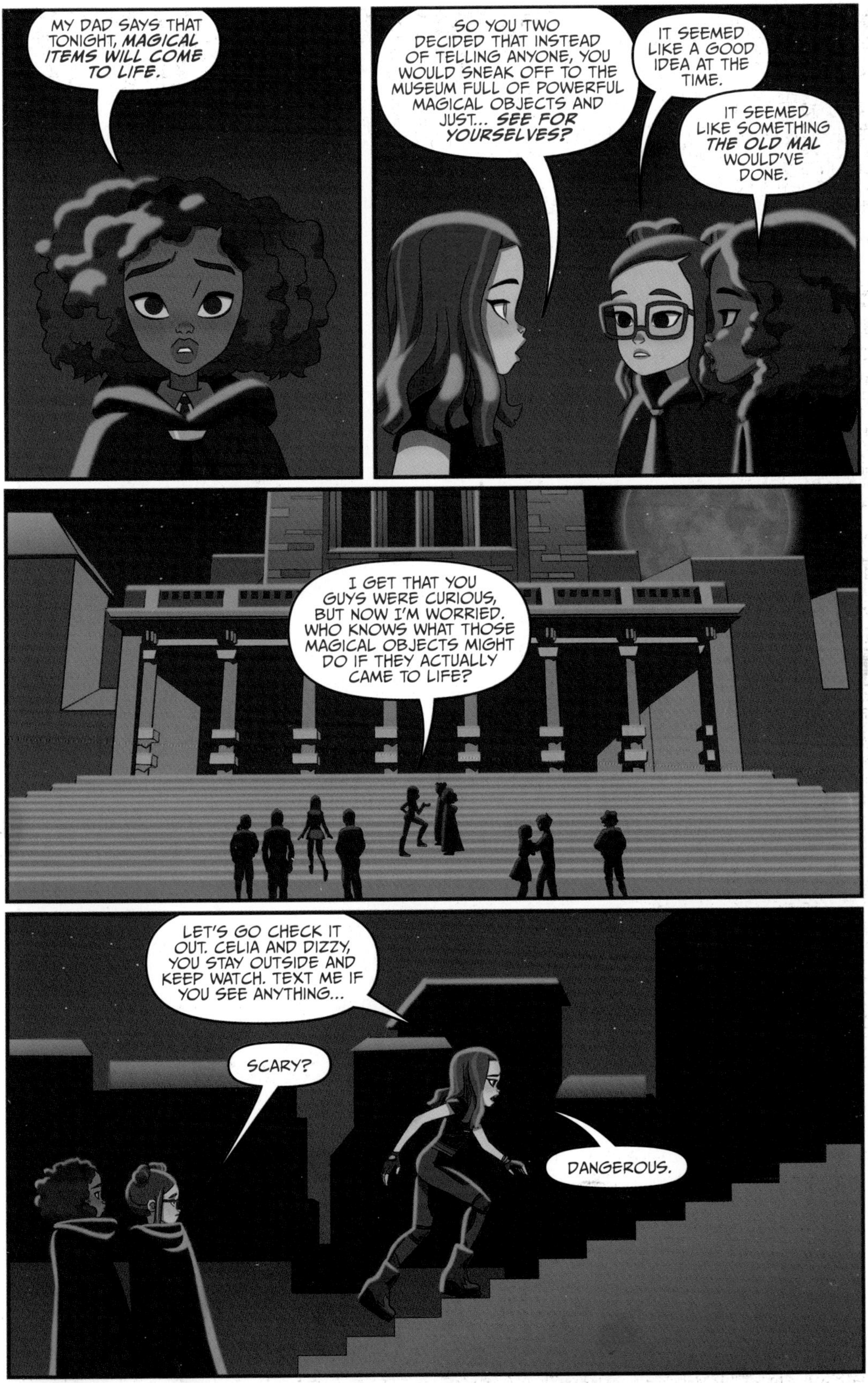
MY DAD SAYS THAT TONIGHT, ***MAGICAL ITEMS WILL COME TO LIFE.***
SO YOU TWO DECIDED THAT INSTEAD OF TELLING ANYONE, YOU WOULD SNEAK OFF TO THE MUSEUM FULL OF POWERFUL MAGICAL OBJECTS AND JUST... ***SEE FOR YOURSELVES?***
IT SEEMED LIKE A GOOD IDEA AT THE TIME.
IT SEEMED LIKE SOMETHING ***THE OLD MAL*** WOULD'VE DONE.
I GET THAT YOU GUYS WERE CURIOUS, BUT NOW I'M WORRIED. WHO KNOWS WHAT THOSE MAGICAL OBJECTS MIGHT DO IF THEY ACTUALLY CAME TO LIFE?
LET'S GO CHECK IT OUT. CELIA AND DIZZY, YOU STAY OUTSIDE AND KEEP WATCH. TEXT ME IF YOU SEE ANYTHING...
SCARY?
DANGEROUS.

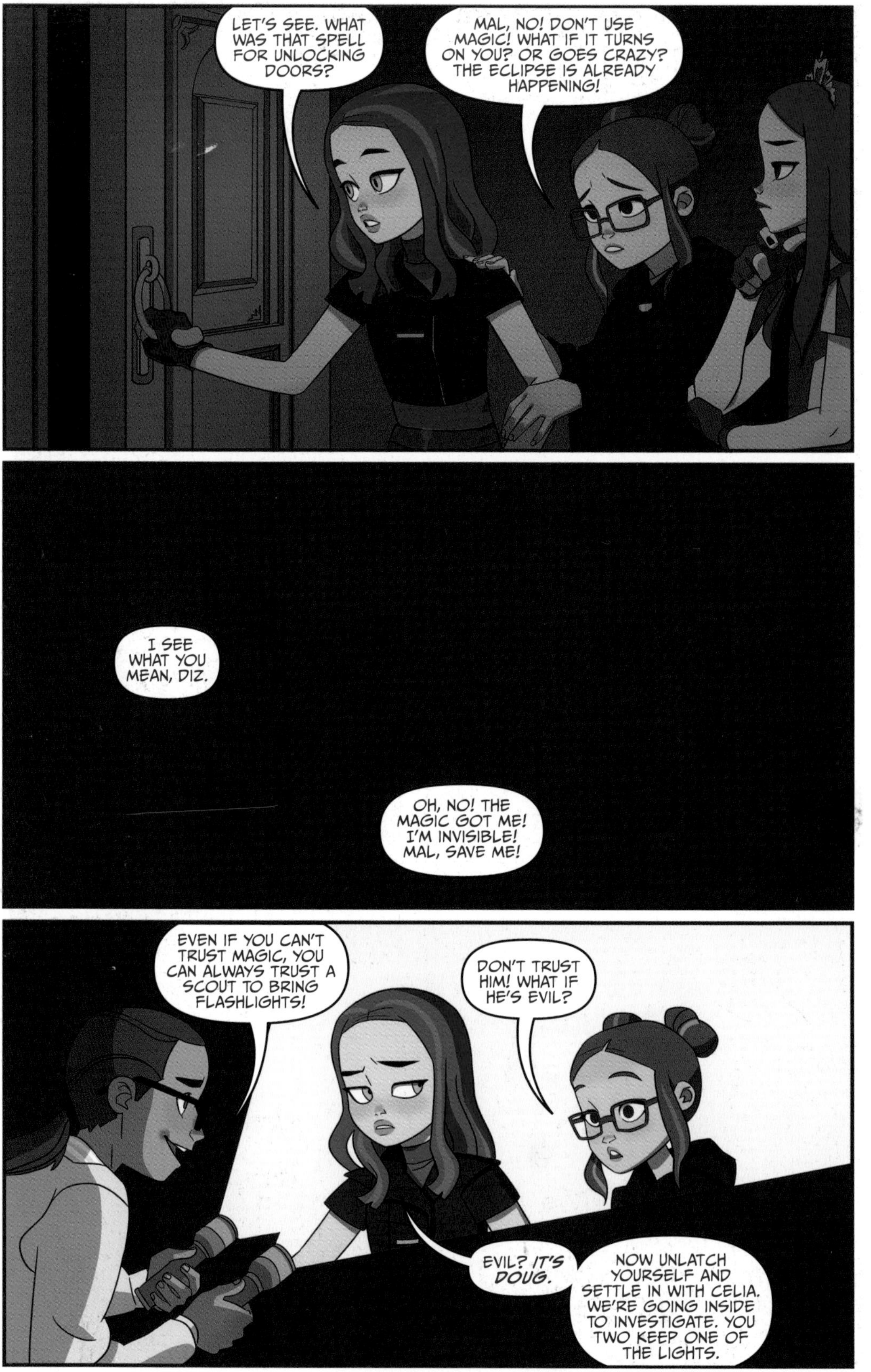
LET'S SEE. WHAT WAS THAT SPELL FOR UNLOCKING DOORS?
MAL, NO! DON'T USE MAGIC! WHAT IF IT TURNS ON YOU? OR GOES CRAZY? THE ECLIPSE IS ALREADY HAPPENING!
I SEE WHAT YOU MEAN, DIZ.
OH, NO! THE MAGIC GOT ME! I'M INVISIBLE! MAL, SAVE ME!
EVEN IF YOU CAN'T TRUST MAGIC, YOU CAN ALWAYS TRUST A SCOUT TO BRING FLASHLIGHTS!
DON'T TRUST HIM! WHAT IF HE'S EVIL?
EVIL? *IT'S DOUG.*
NOW UNLATCH YOURSELF AND SETTLE IN WITH CELIA. WE'RE GOING INSIDE TO INVESTIGATE. YOU TWO KEEP ONE OF THE LIGHTS.

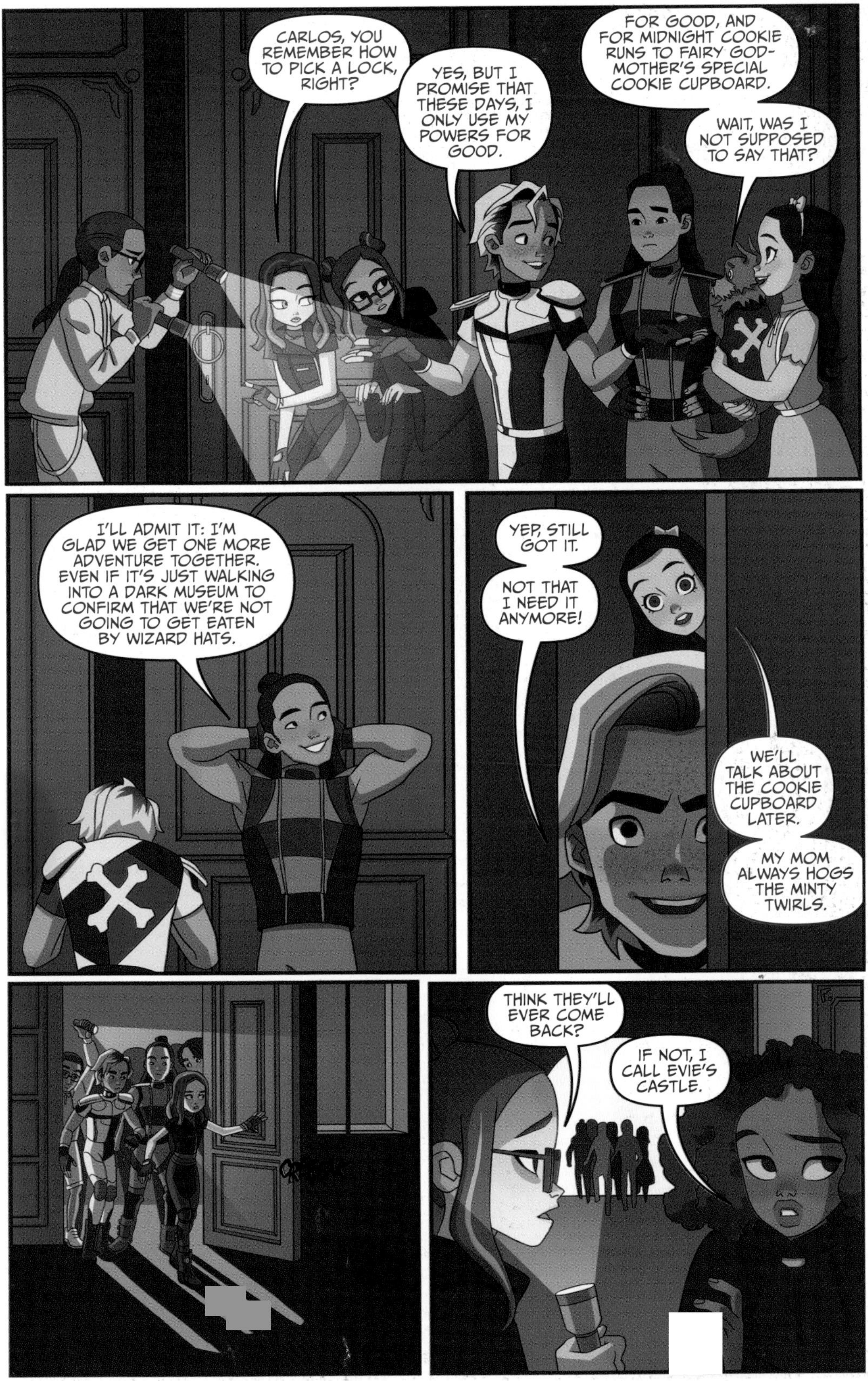
CARLOS, YOU REMEMBER HOW TO PICK A LOCK, RIGHT?
YES, BUT I PROMISE THAT THESE DAYS, I ONLY USE MY POWERS FOR GOOD.
FOR GOOD, AND FOR MIDNIGHT COOKIE RUNS TO FAIRY GOD-MOTHER'S SPECIAL COOKIE CUPBOARD.
WAIT, WAS I NOT SUPPOSED TO SAY THAT?
I'LL ADMIT IT: I'M GLAD WE GET ONE MORE ADVENTURE TOGETHER. EVEN IF IT'S JUST WALKING INTO A DARK MUSEUM TO CONFIRM THAT WE'RE NOT GOING TO GET EATEN BY WIZARD HATS.
YEP, STILL GOT IT.
NOT THAT I NEED IT ANYMORE!
WE'LL TALK ABOUT THE COOKIE CUPBOARD LATER.
MY MOM ALWAYS HOGS THE MINTY TWIRLS.
THINK THEY'LL EVER COME BACK?
IF NOT, I CALL EVIE'S CASTLE.

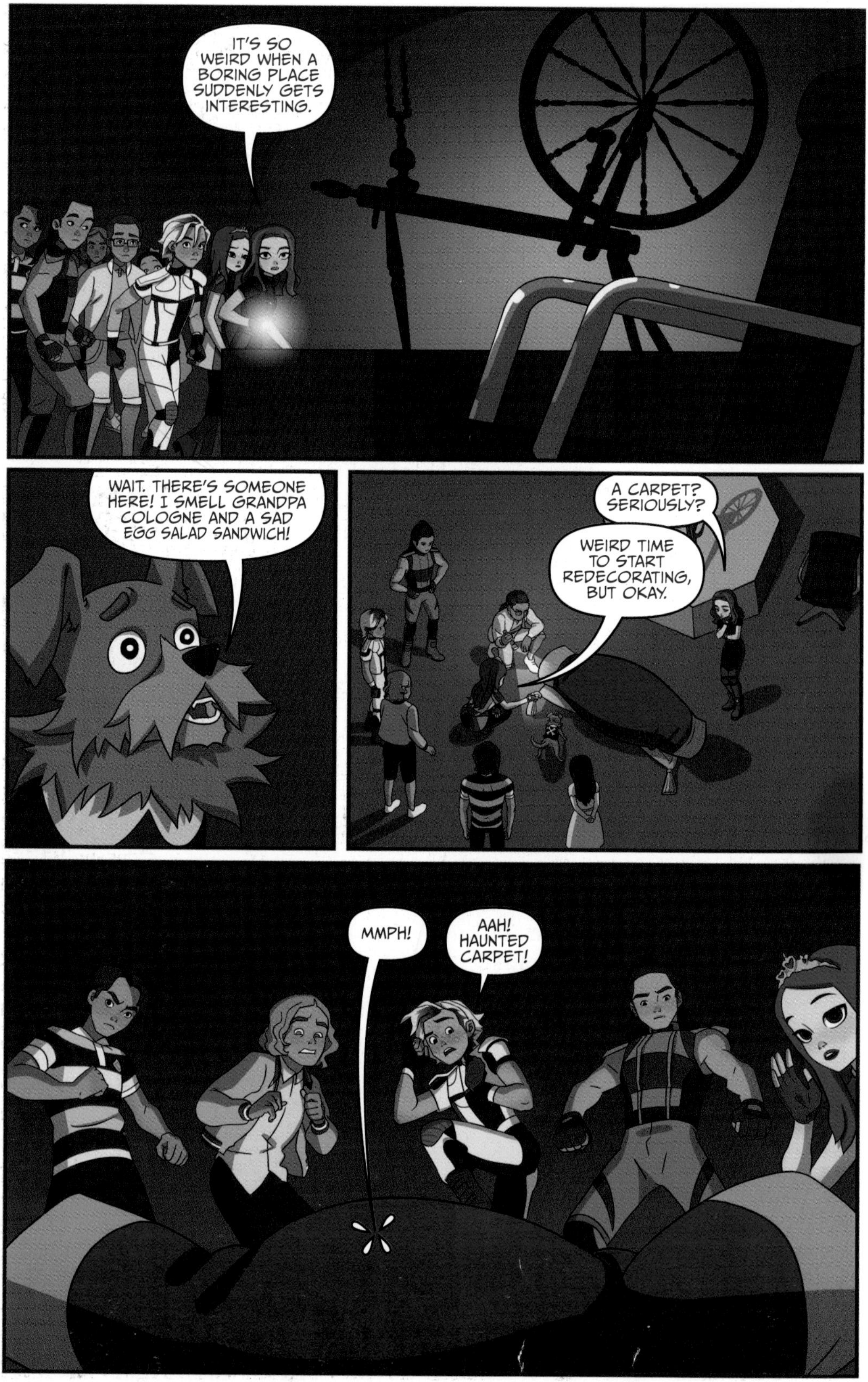
IT'S SO WEIRD WHEN A BORING PLACE SUDDENLY GETS INTERESTING.
WAIT. THERE'S SOMEONE HERE! I SMELL GRANDPA COLOGNE AND A SAD EGG SALAD SANDWICH!
A CARPET? SERIOUSLY?
WEIRD TIME TO START REDECORATING, BUT OKAY.
MMPH!
AAH! HAUNTED CARPET!

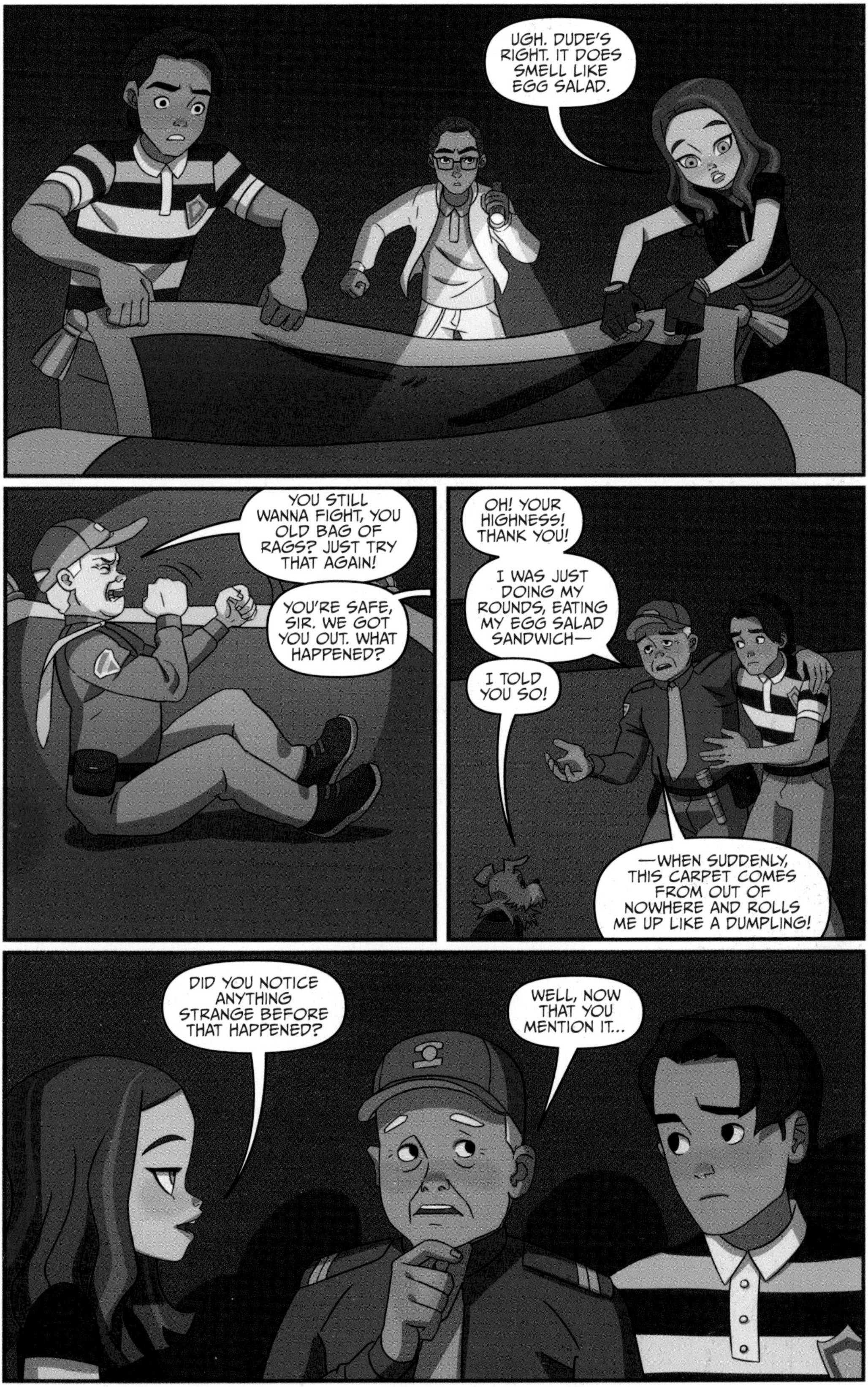
UGH. DUDE'S RIGHT. IT DOES SMELL LIKE EGG SALAD.
YOU STILL WANNA FIGHT, YOU OLD BAG OF RAGS? JUST TRY THAT AGAIN!
YOU'RE SAFE, SIR. WE GOT YOU OUT. WHAT HAPPENED?
OH! YOUR HIGHNESS! THANK YOU!
I WAS JUST DOING MY ROUNDS, EATING MY EGG SALAD SANDWICH—
I TOLD YOU SO!
—WHEN SUDDENLY, THIS CARPET COMES FROM OUT OF NOWHERE AND ROLLS ME UP LIKE A DUMPLING!
DID YOU NOTICE ANYTHING STRANGE BEFORE THAT HAPPENED?
WELL, NOW THAT YOU MENTION IT...

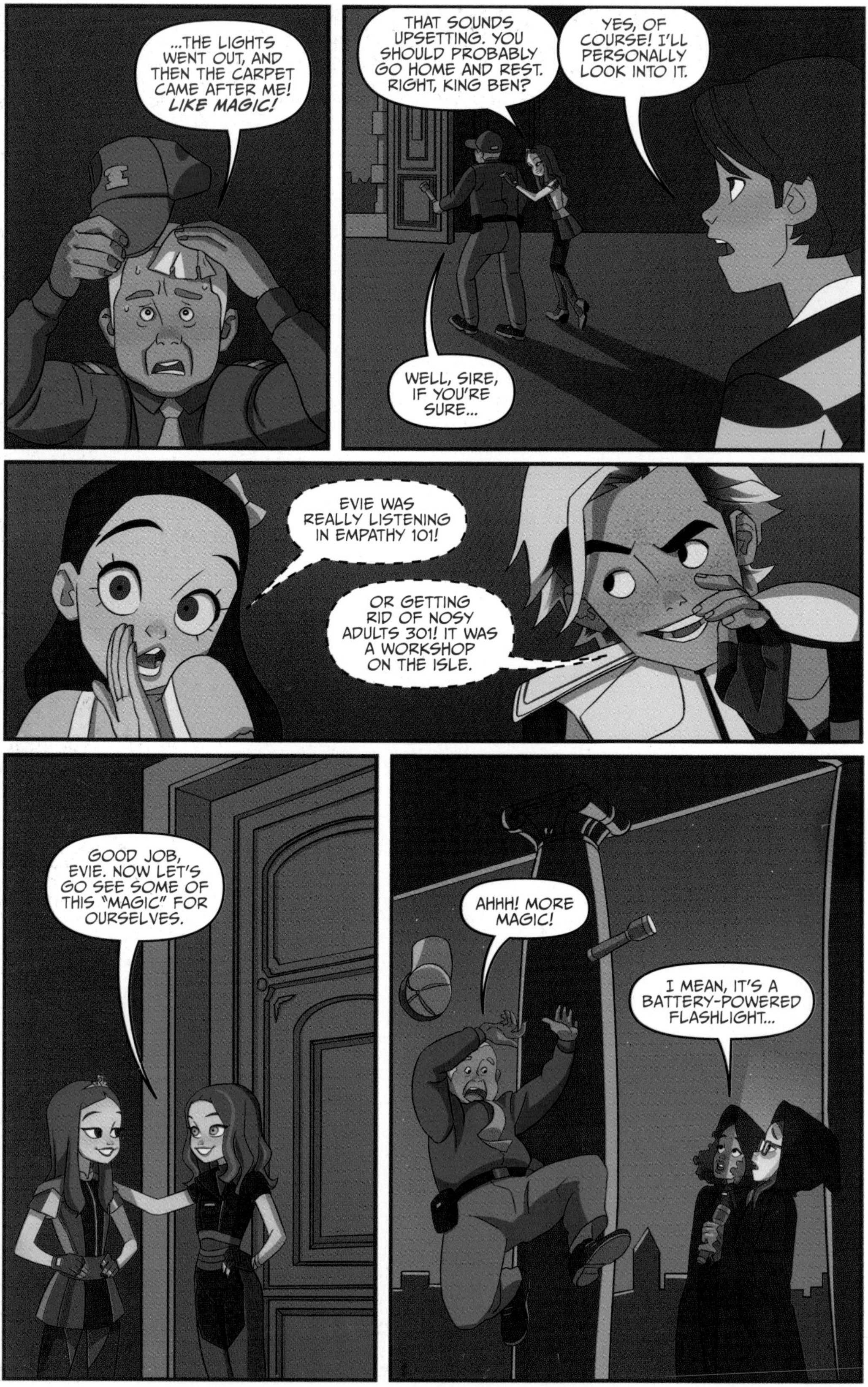
...THE LIGHTS WENT OUT, AND THEN THE CARPET CAME AFTER ME! LIKE MAGIC!
THAT SOUNDS UPSETTING. YOU SHOULD PROBABLY GO HOME AND REST. RIGHT, KING BEN?
YES, OF COURSE! I'LL PERSONALLY LOOK INTO IT.
WELL, SIRE, IF YOU'RE SURE...
EVIE WAS REALLY LISTENING IN EMPATHY 101!
OR GETTING RID OF NOSY ADULTS 301! IT WAS A WORKSHOP ON THE ISLE.
GOOD JOB, EVIE. NOW LET'S GO SEE SOME OF THIS "MAGIC" FOR OURSELVES.
AHHH! MORE MAGIC!
I MEAN, IT'S A BATTERY-POWERED FLASHLIGHT...

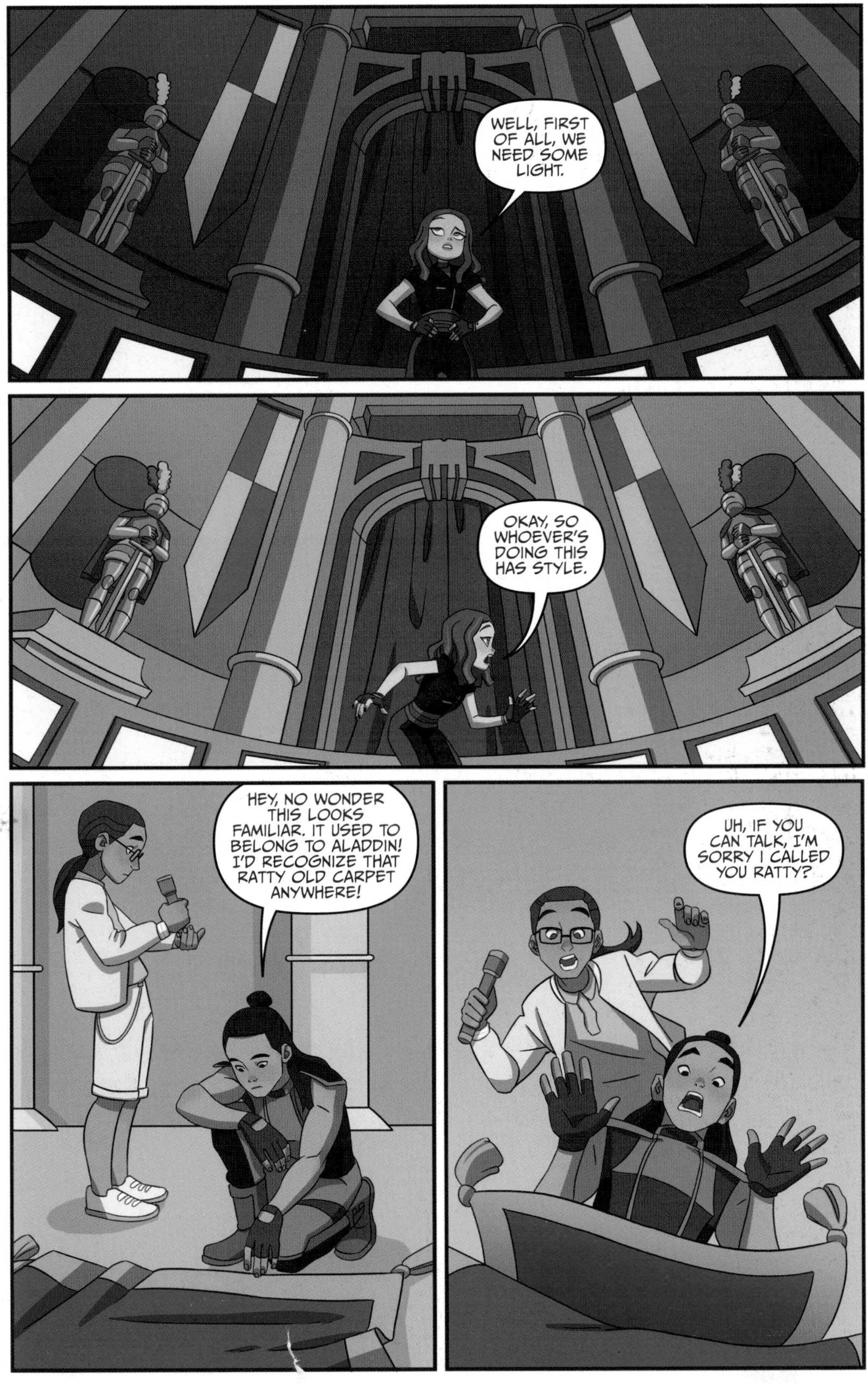
WELL, FIRST OF ALL, WE NEED SOME LIGHT.
OKAY, SO WHOEVER'S DOING THIS HAS STYLE.
HEY, NO WONDER THIS LOOKS FAMILIAR. IT USED TO BELONG TO ALADDIN! I'D RECOGNIZE THAT RATTY OLD CARPET ANYWHERE!
UH, IF YOU CAN TALK, I'M SORRY I CALLED YOU RATTY?

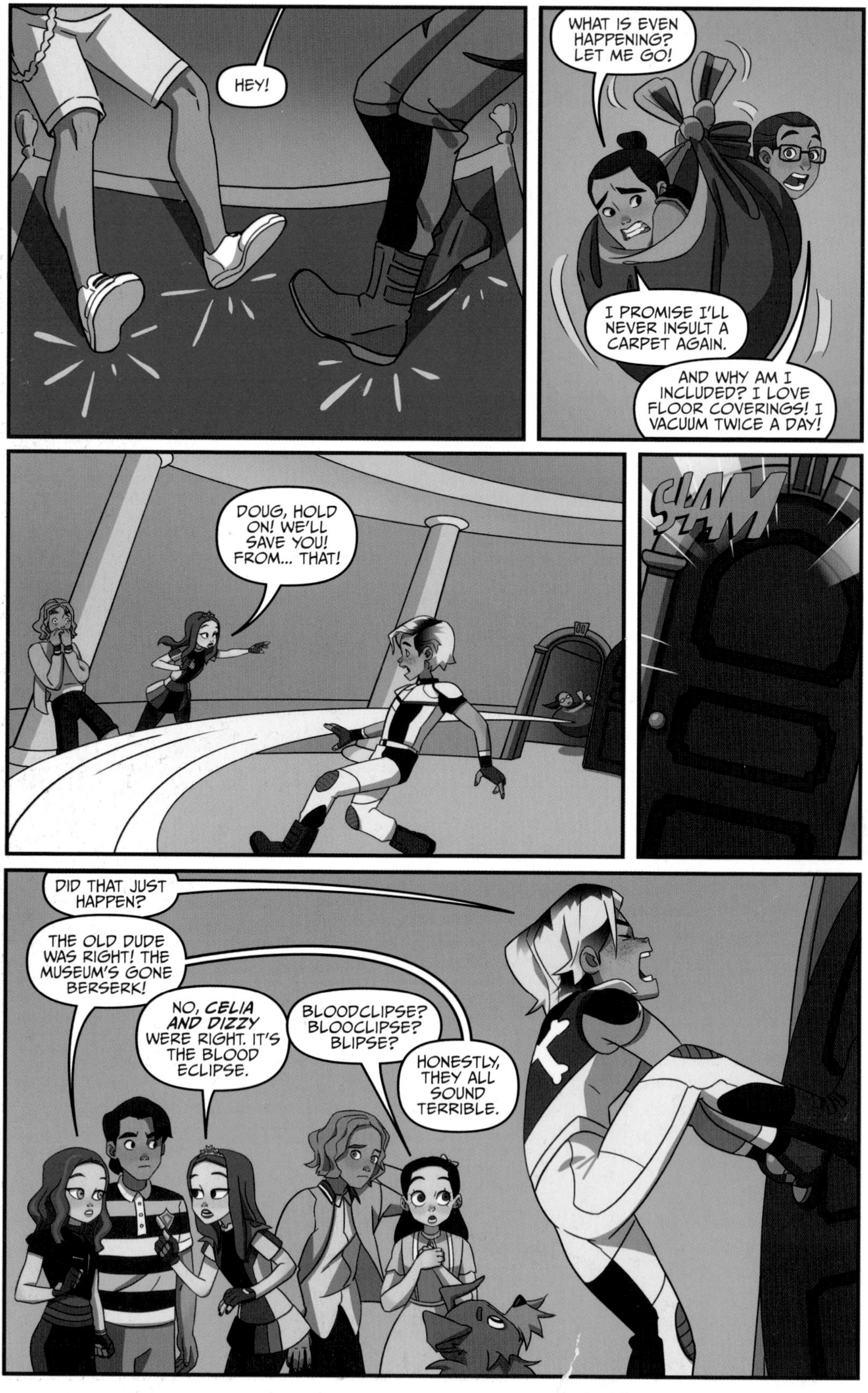
HEY!
WHAT IS EVEN HAPPENING? LET ME GO!
I PROMISE I'LL NEVER INSULT A CARPET AGAIN.
AND WHY AM I INCLUDED? I LOVE FLOOR COVERINGS! I VACUUM TWICE A DAY!
DOUG, HOLD ON! WE'LL SAVE YOU! FROM... THAT!
SLAM
DID THAT JUST HAPPEN?
THE OLD DUDE WAS RIGHT! THE MUSEUM'S GONE BERSERK!
NO, *CELIA AND DIZZY* WERE RIGHT. IT'S THE BLOOD ECLIPSE.
BLOODCLIPSE? BLOOCLIPSE? BLIPSE?
HONESTLY, THEY ALL SOUND TERRIBLE.

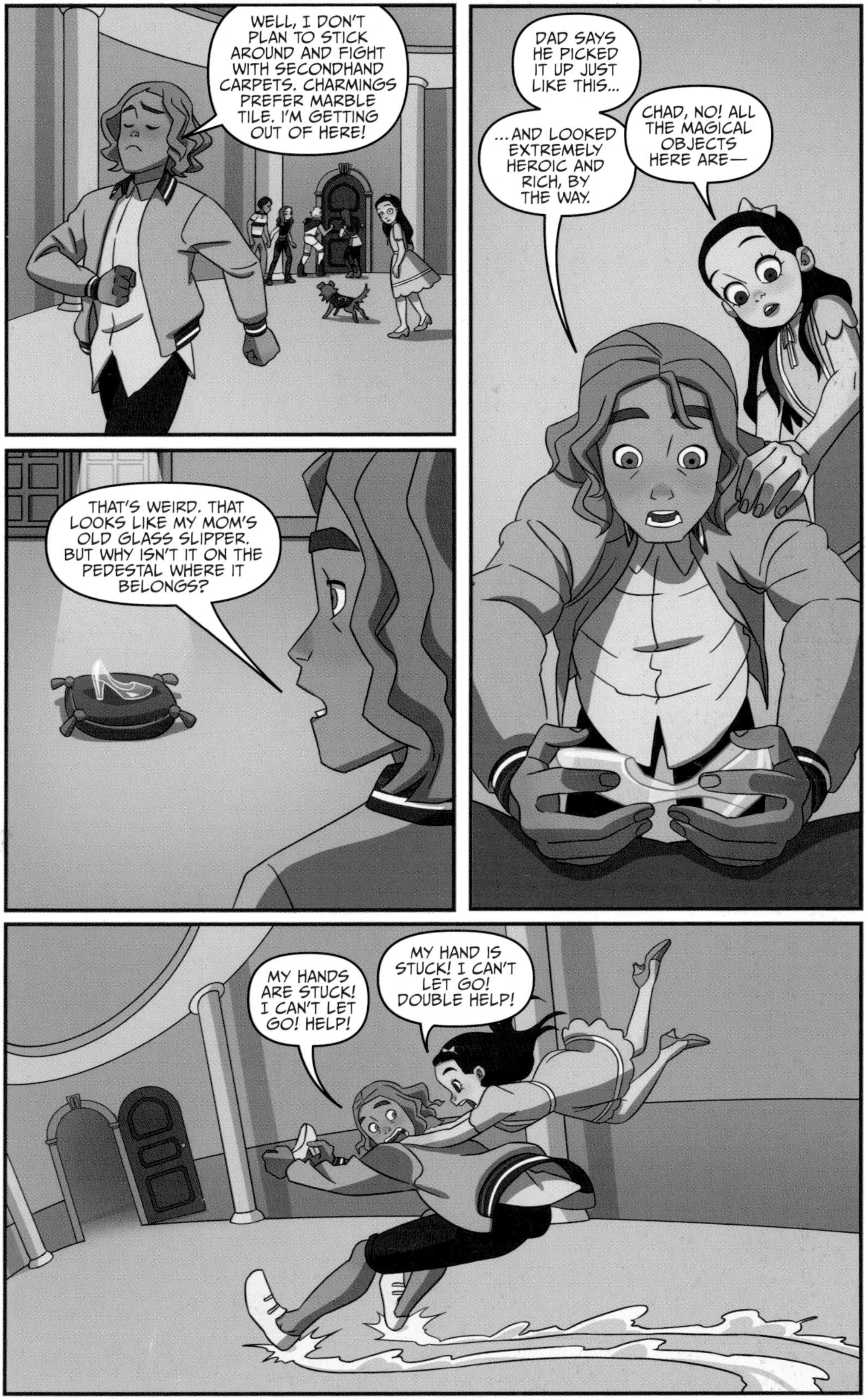
WELL, I DON'T PLAN TO STICK AROUND AND FIGHT WITH SECONDHAND CARPETS. CHARMINGS PREFER MARBLE TILE. I'M GETTING OUT OF HERE!
DAD SAYS HE PICKED IT UP JUST LIKE THIS...
...AND LOOKED EXTREMELY HEROIC AND RICH, BY THE WAY.
CHAD, NO! ALL THE MAGICAL OBJECTS HERE ARE—
THAT'S WEIRD. THAT LOOKS LIKE MY MOM'S OLD GLASS SLIPPER. BUT WHY ISN'T IT ON THE PEDESTAL WHERE IT BELONGS?
MY HANDS ARE STUCK! I CAN'T LET GO! HELP!
MY HAND IS STUCK! I CAN'T LET GO! DOUBLE HELP!

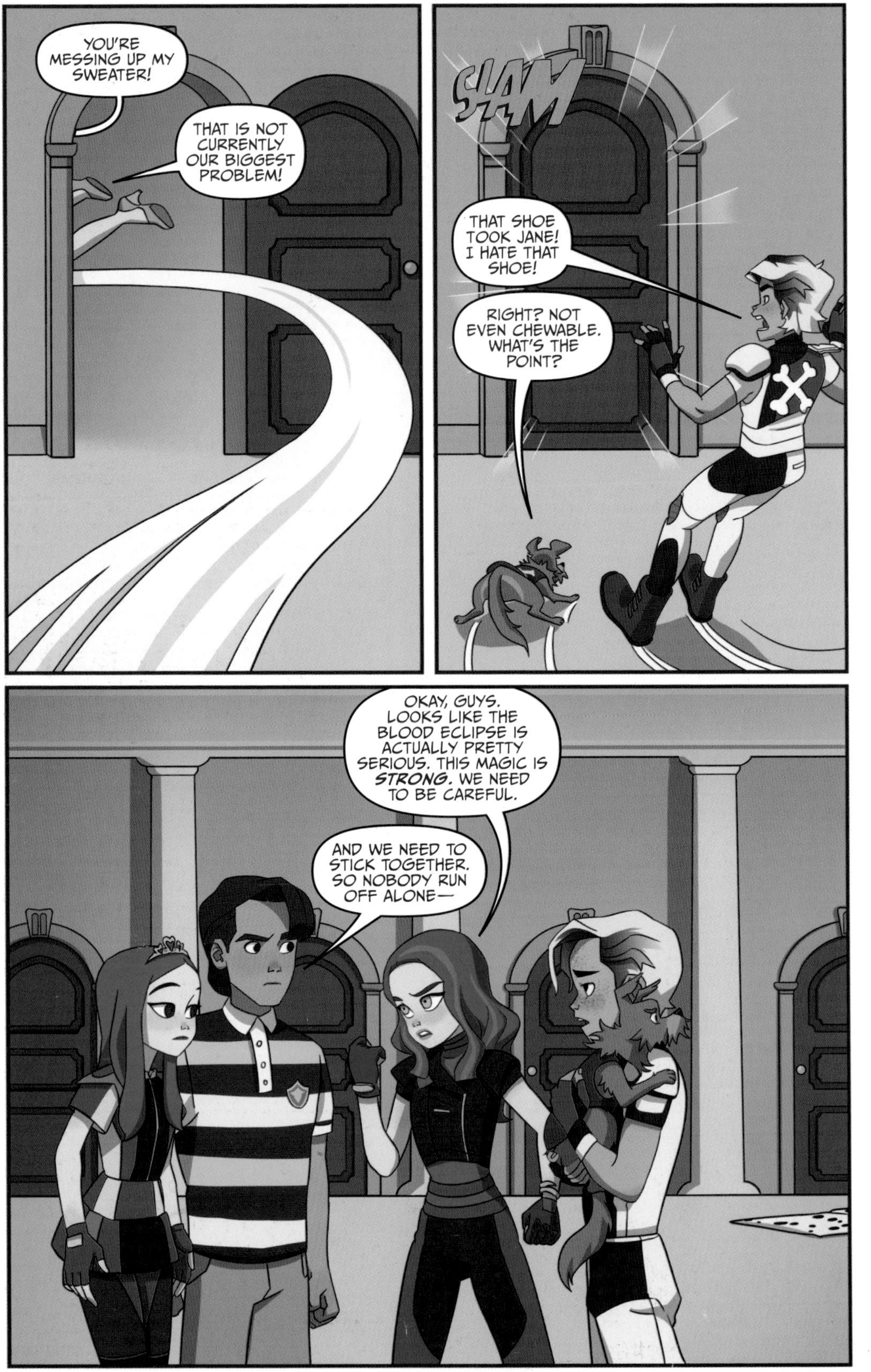
YOU'RE MESSING UP MY SWEATER!
THAT IS NOT CURRENTLY OUR BIGGEST PROBLEM!
SLAM
THAT SHOE TOOK JANE! I HATE THAT SHOE!
RIGHT? NOT EVEN CHEWABLE. WHAT'S THE POINT?
OKAY, GUYS. LOOKS LIKE THE BLOOD ECLIPSE IS ACTUALLY PRETTY SERIOUS. THIS MAGIC IS ***STRONG.*** WE NEED TO BE CAREFUL.
AND WE NEED TO STICK TOGETHER. SO NOBODY RUN OFF ALONE—

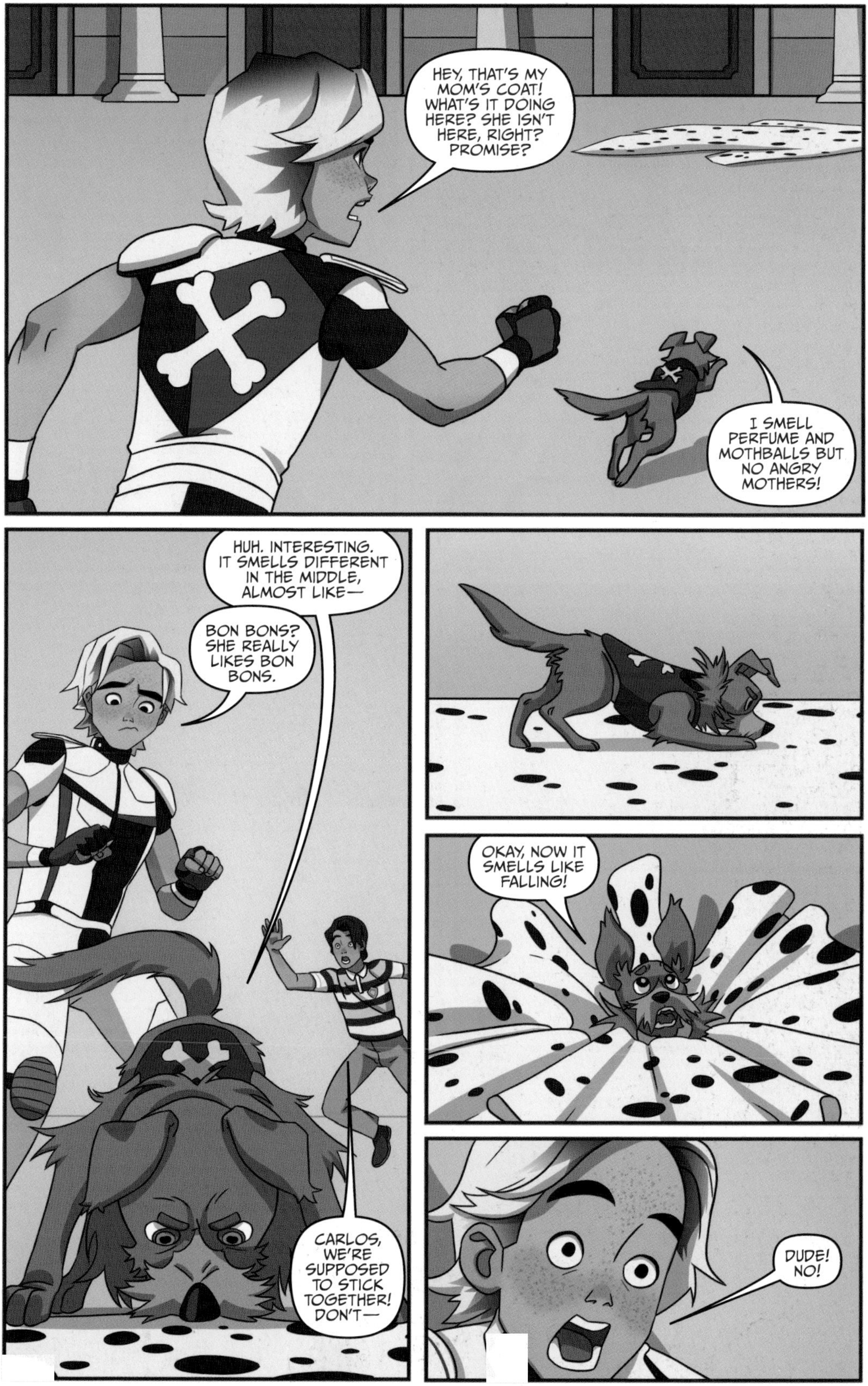
HEY, THAT'S MY MOM'S COAT! WHAT'S IT DOING HERE? SHE ISN'T HERE, RIGHT? PROMISE?
I SMELL PERFUME AND MOTHBALLS BUT NO ANGRY MOTHERS!
HUH. INTERESTING. IT SMELLS DIFFERENT IN THE MIDDLE, ALMOST LIKE—
BON BONS? SHE REALLY LIKES BON BONS.
CARLOS, WE'RE SUPPOSED TO STICK TOGETHER! DON'T—
OKAY, NOW IT SMELLS LIKE FALLING!
DUDE! NO!

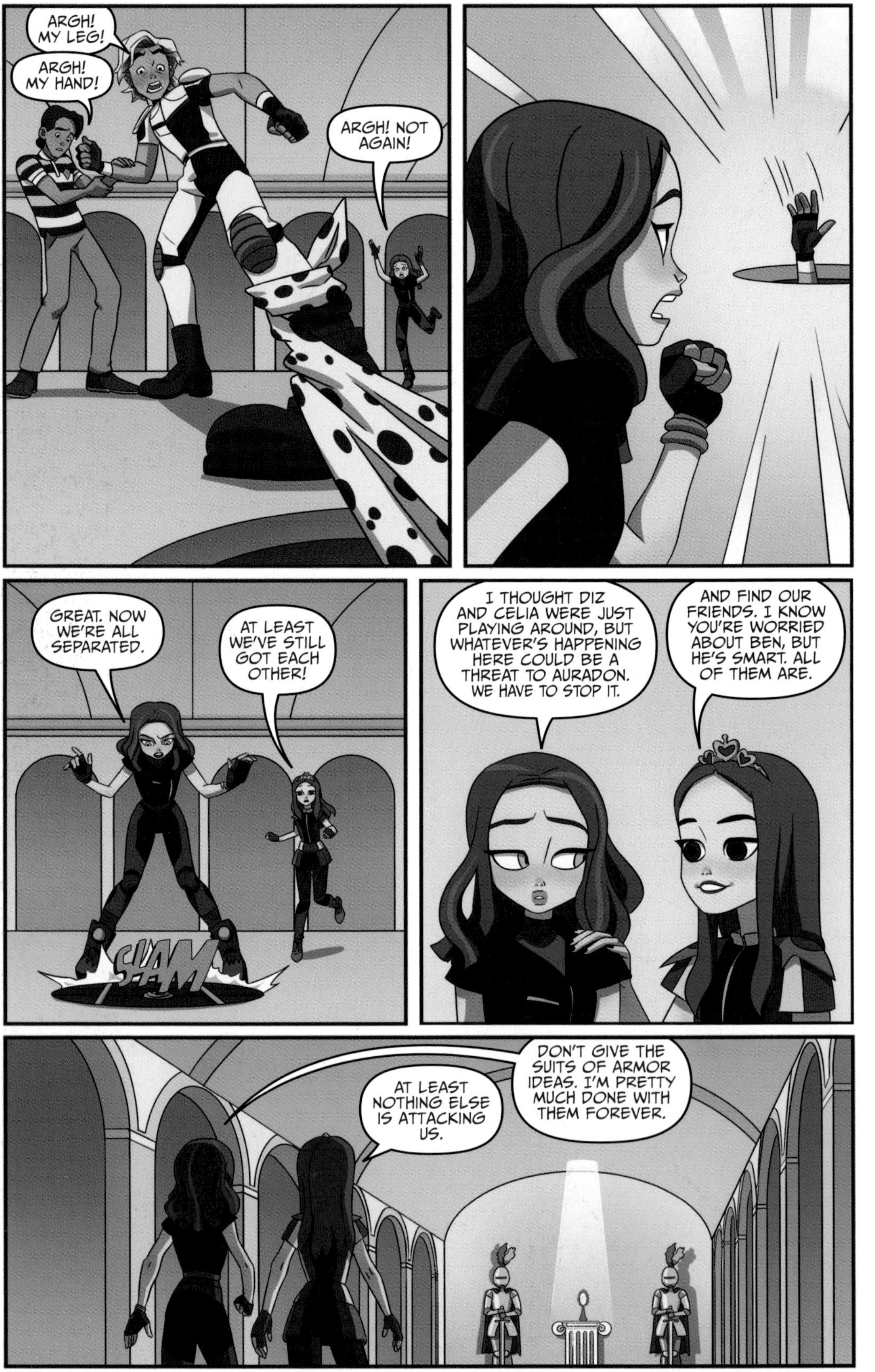
ARGH! MY LEG!
ARGH! MY HAND!
ARGH! NOT AGAIN!
GREAT. NOW WE'RE ALL SEPARATED.
AT LEAST WE'VE STILL GOT EACH OTHER!
SLAM
I THOUGHT DIZ AND CELIA WERE JUST PLAYING AROUND, BUT WHATEVER'S HAPPENING HERE COULD BE A THREAT TO AURADON. WE HAVE TO STOP IT.
AND FIND OUR FRIENDS. I KNOW YOU'RE WORRIED ABOUT BEN, BUT HE'S SMART. ALL OF THEM ARE.
AT LEAST NOTHING ELSE IS ATTACKING US.
DON'T GIVE THE SUITS OF ARMOR IDEAS. I'M PRETTY MUCH DONE WITH THEM FOREVER.

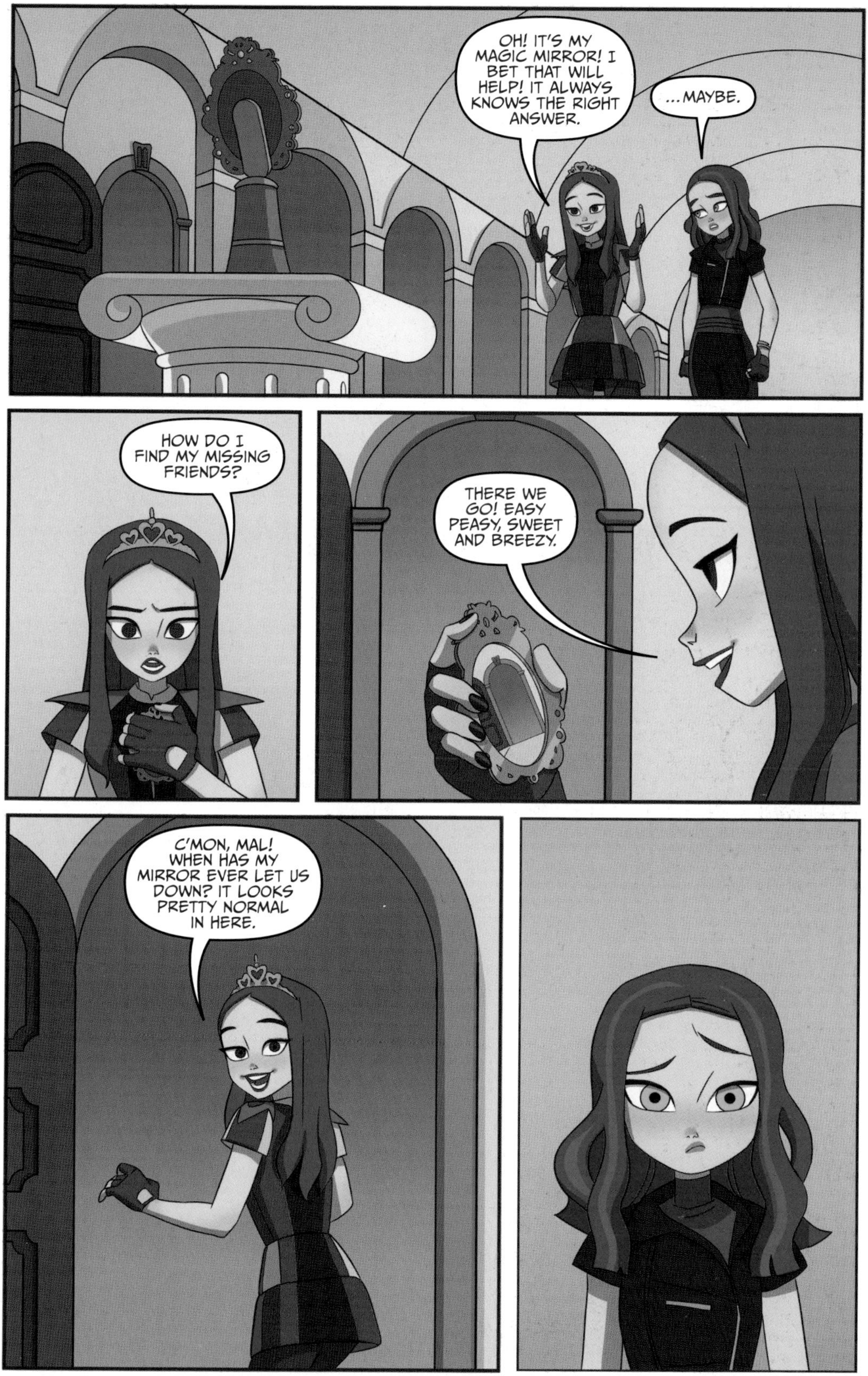
OH! IT'S MY MAGIC MIRROR! I BET THAT WILL HELP! IT ALWAYS KNOWS THE RIGHT ANSWER.
...MAYBE.
HOW DO I FIND MY MISSING FRIENDS?
THERE WE GO! EASY PEASY, SWEET AND BREEZY.
C'MON, MAL! WHEN HAS MY MIRROR EVER LET US DOWN? IT LOOKS PRETTY NORMAL IN HERE.

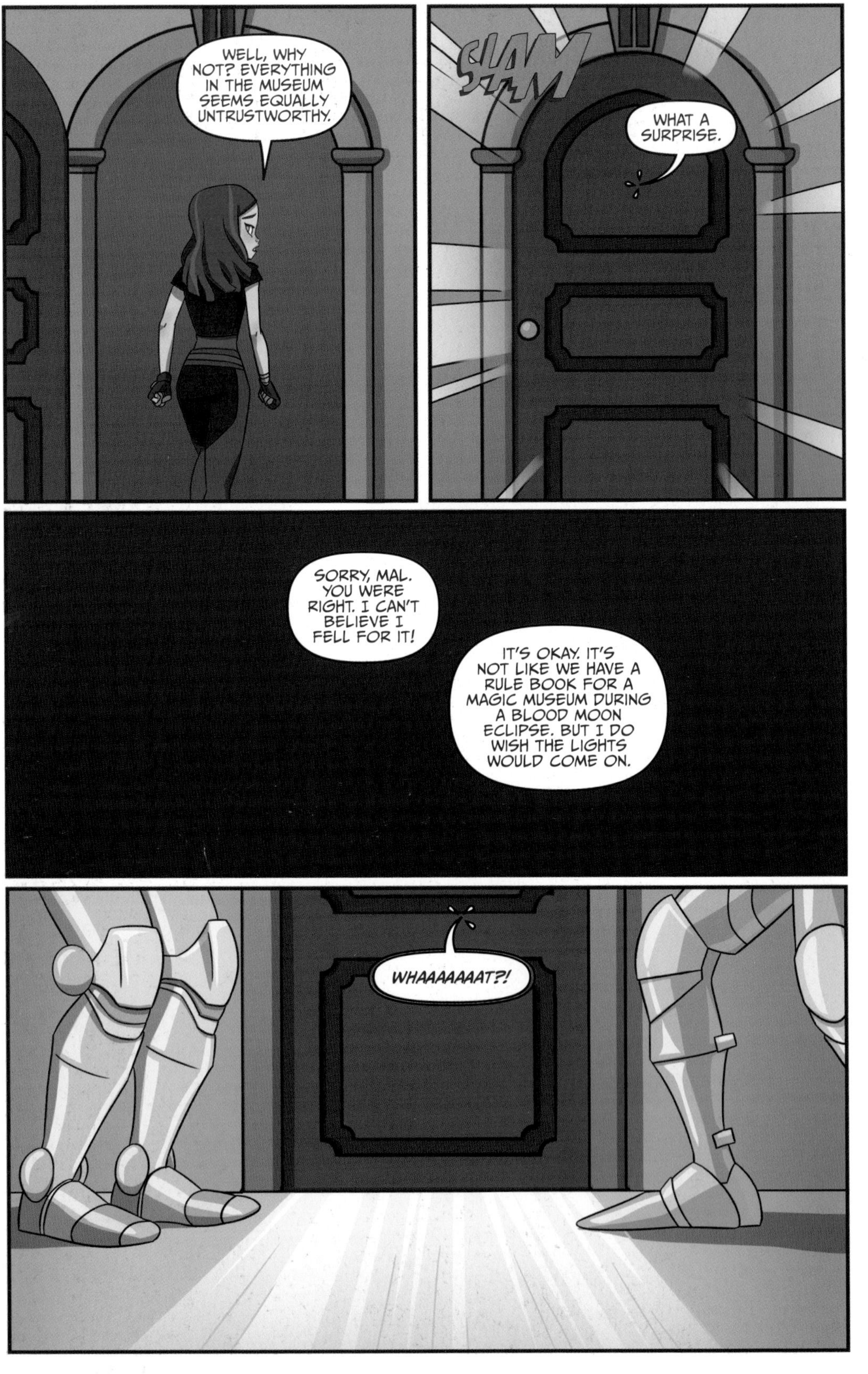
WELL, WHY NOT? EVERYTHING IN THE MUSEUM SEEMS EQUALLY UNTRUSTWORTHY.
SLAM
WHAT A SURPRISE.
SORRY, MAL. YOU WERE RIGHT. I CAN'T BELIEVE I FELL FOR IT!
IT'S OKAY. IT'S NOT LIKE WE HAVE A RULE BOOK FOR A MAGIC MUSEUM DURING A BLOOD MOON ECLIPSE. BUT I DO WISH THE LIGHTS WOULD COME ON.
WHAAAAAAAT?!

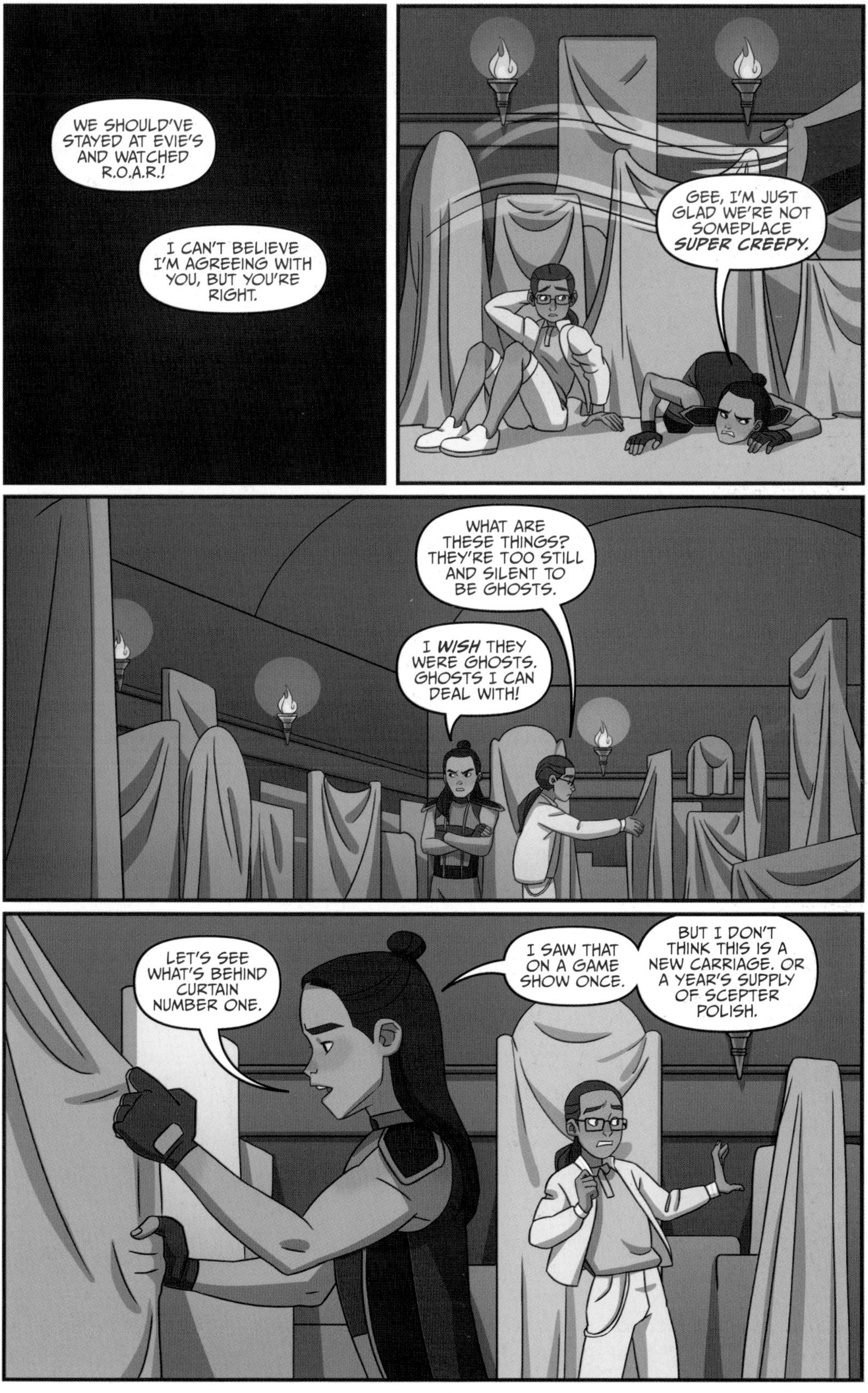
WE SHOULD'VE STAYED AT EVIE'S AND WATCHED R.O.A.R.!
I CAN'T BELIEVE I'M AGREEING WITH YOU, BUT YOU'RE RIGHT.
GEE, I'M JUST GLAD WE'RE NOT SOMEPLACE SUPER CREEPY.
WHAT ARE THESE THINGS? THEY'RE TOO STILL AND SILENT TO BE GHOSTS.
I WISH THEY WERE GHOSTS. GHOSTS I CAN DEAL WITH!
LET'S SEE WHAT'S BEHIND CURTAIN NUMBER ONE.
I SAW THAT ON A GAME SHOW ONCE.
BUT I DON'T THINK THIS IS A NEW CARRIAGE. OR A YEAR'S SUPPLY OF SCEPTER POLISH.

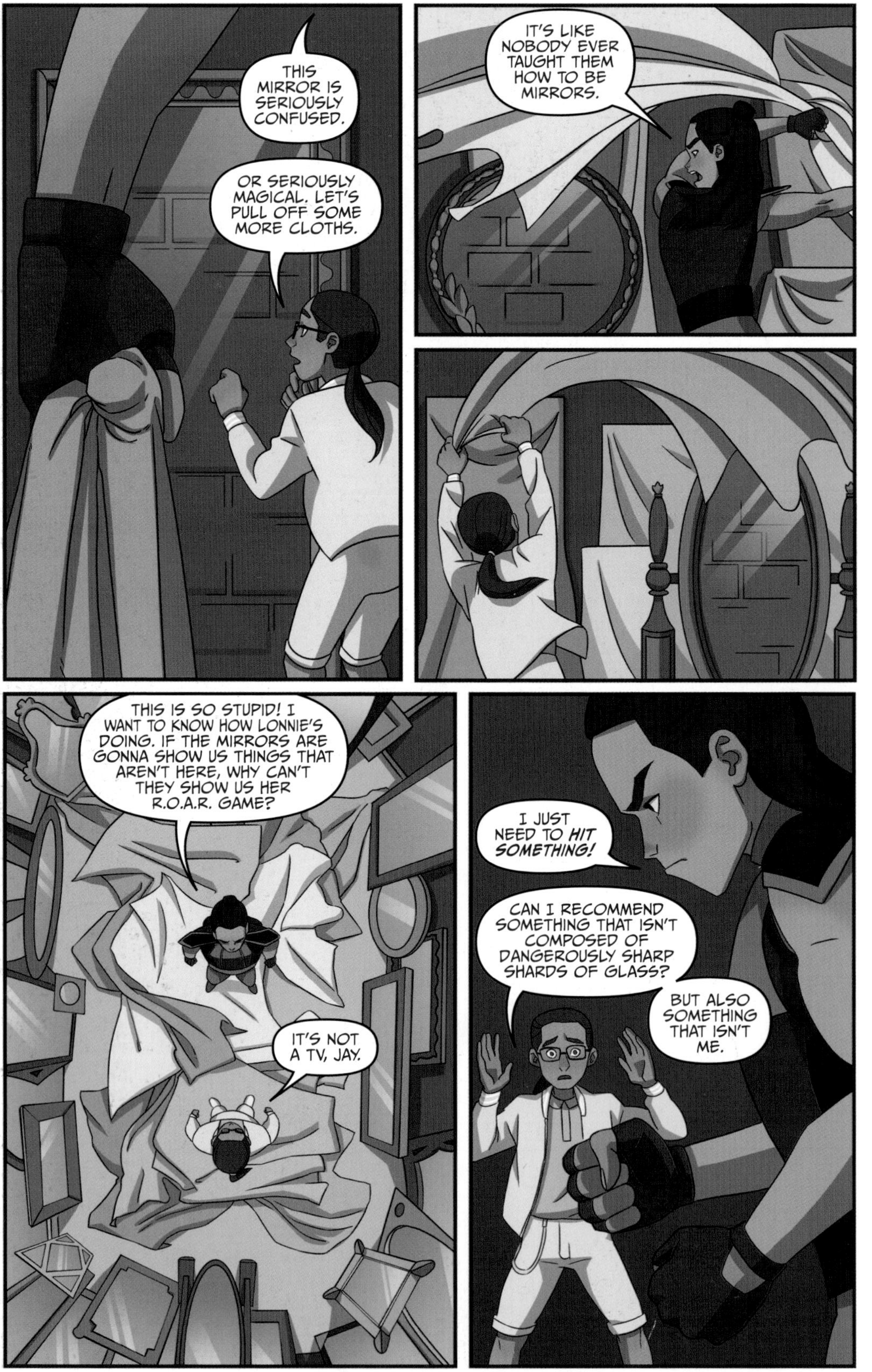
THIS MIRROR IS SERIOUSLY CONFUSED.
OR SERIOUSLY MAGICAL. LET'S PULL OFF SOME MORE CLOTHS.
IT'S LIKE NOBODY EVER TAUGHT THEM HOW TO BE MIRRORS.
THIS IS SO STUPID! I WANT TO KNOW HOW LONNIE'S DOING. IF THE MIRRORS ARE GONNA SHOW US THINGS THAT AREN'T HERE, WHY CAN'T THEY SHOW US HER R.O.A.R. GAME?
IT'S NOT A TV, JAY.
I JUST NEED TO *HIT SOMETHING!*
CAN I RECOMMEND SOMETHING THAT ISN'T COMPOSED OF DANGEROUSLY SHARP SHARDS OF GLASS?
BUT ALSO SOMETHING THAT ISN'T ME.

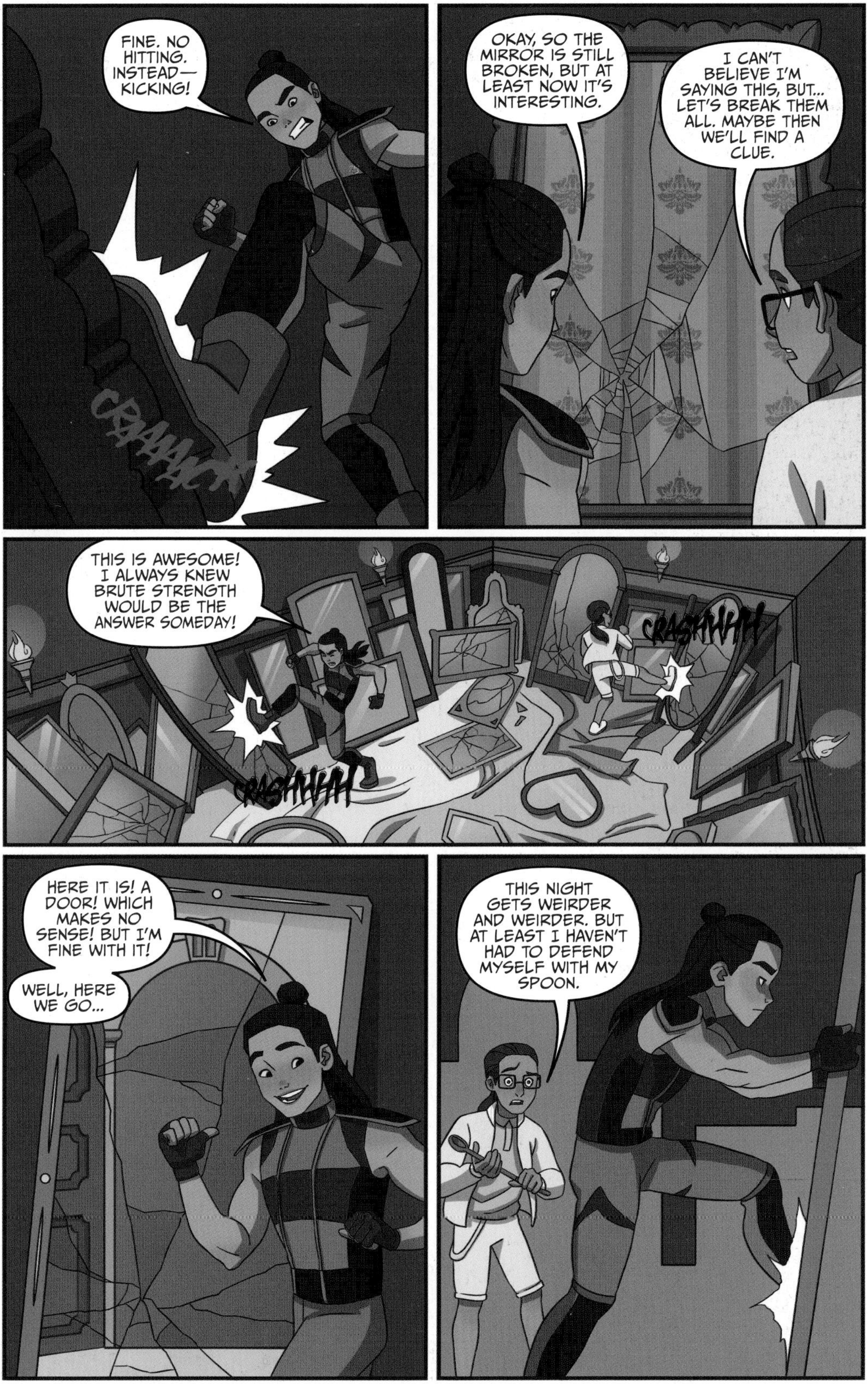
FINE. NO HITTING. INSTEAD— KICKING!
CRAAAACK
OKAY, SO THE MIRROR IS STILL BROKEN, BUT AT LEAST NOW IT'S INTERESTING.
I CAN'T BELIEVE I'M SAYING THIS, BUT... LET'S BREAK THEM ALL. MAYBE THEN WE'LL FIND A CLUE.
THIS IS AWESOME! I ALWAYS KNEW BRUTE STRENGTH WOULD BE THE ANSWER SOMEDAY!
CRASHHHH
CRASHHHH
HERE IT IS! A DOOR! WHICH MAKES NO SENSE! BUT I'M FINE WITH IT!
WELL, HERE WE GO...
THIS NIGHT GETS WEIRDER AND WEIRDER. BUT AT LEAST I HAVEN'T HAD TO DEFEND MYSELF WITH MY SPOON.

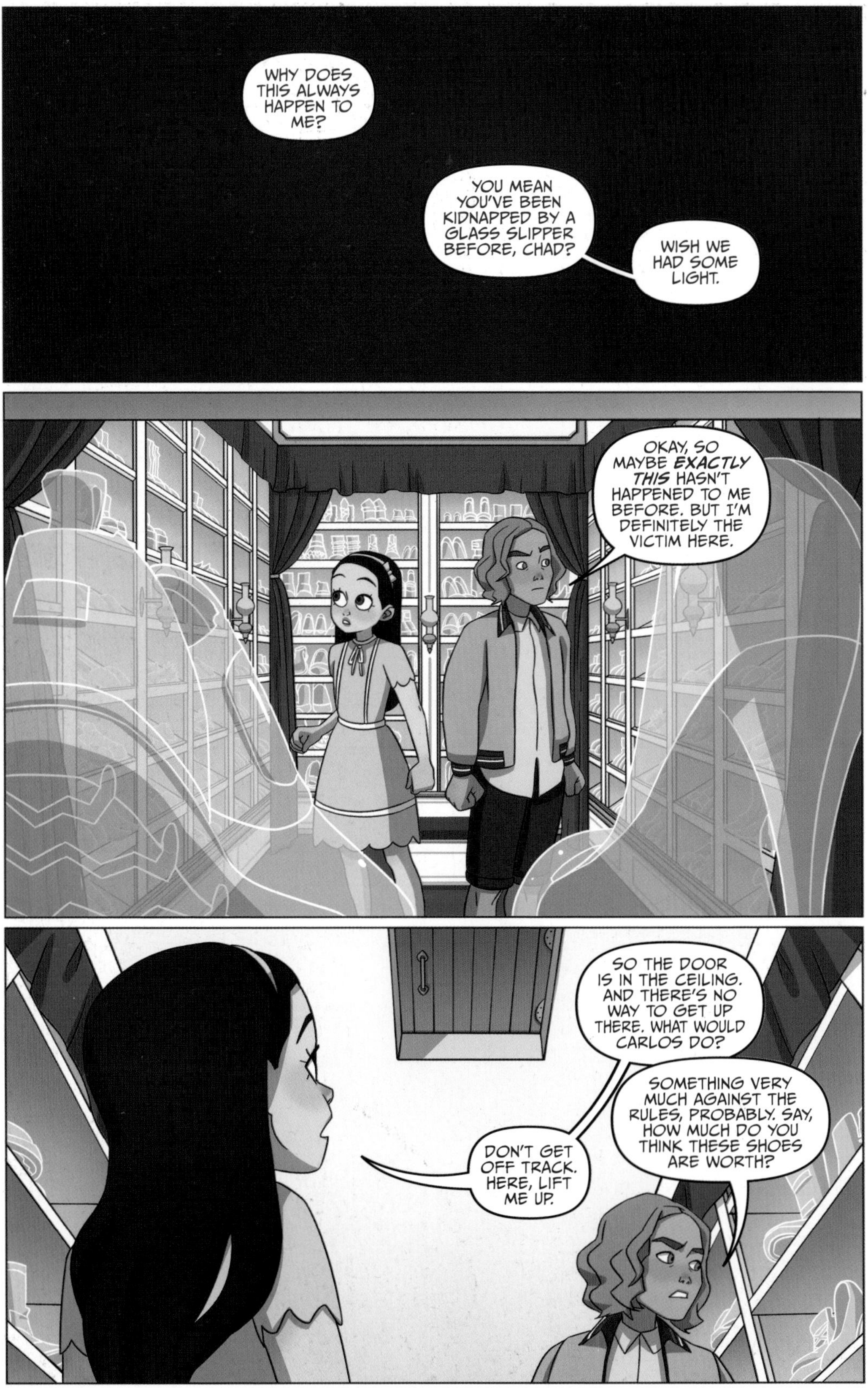
WHY DOES THIS ALWAYS HAPPEN TO ME?
YOU MEAN YOU'VE BEEN KIDNAPPED BY A GLASS SLIPPER BEFORE, CHAD?
WISH WE HAD SOME LIGHT.
OKAY, SO MAYBE ***EXACTLY THIS*** HASN'T HAPPENED TO ME BEFORE. BUT I'M DEFINITELY THE VICTIM HERE.
SO THE DOOR IS IN THE CEILING. AND THERE'S NO WAY TO GET UP THERE. WHAT WOULD CARLOS DO?
SOMETHING VERY MUCH AGAINST THE RULES, PROBABLY. SAY, HOW MUCH DO YOU THINK THESE SHOES ARE WORTH?
DON'T GET OFF TRACK. HERE, LIFT ME UP.

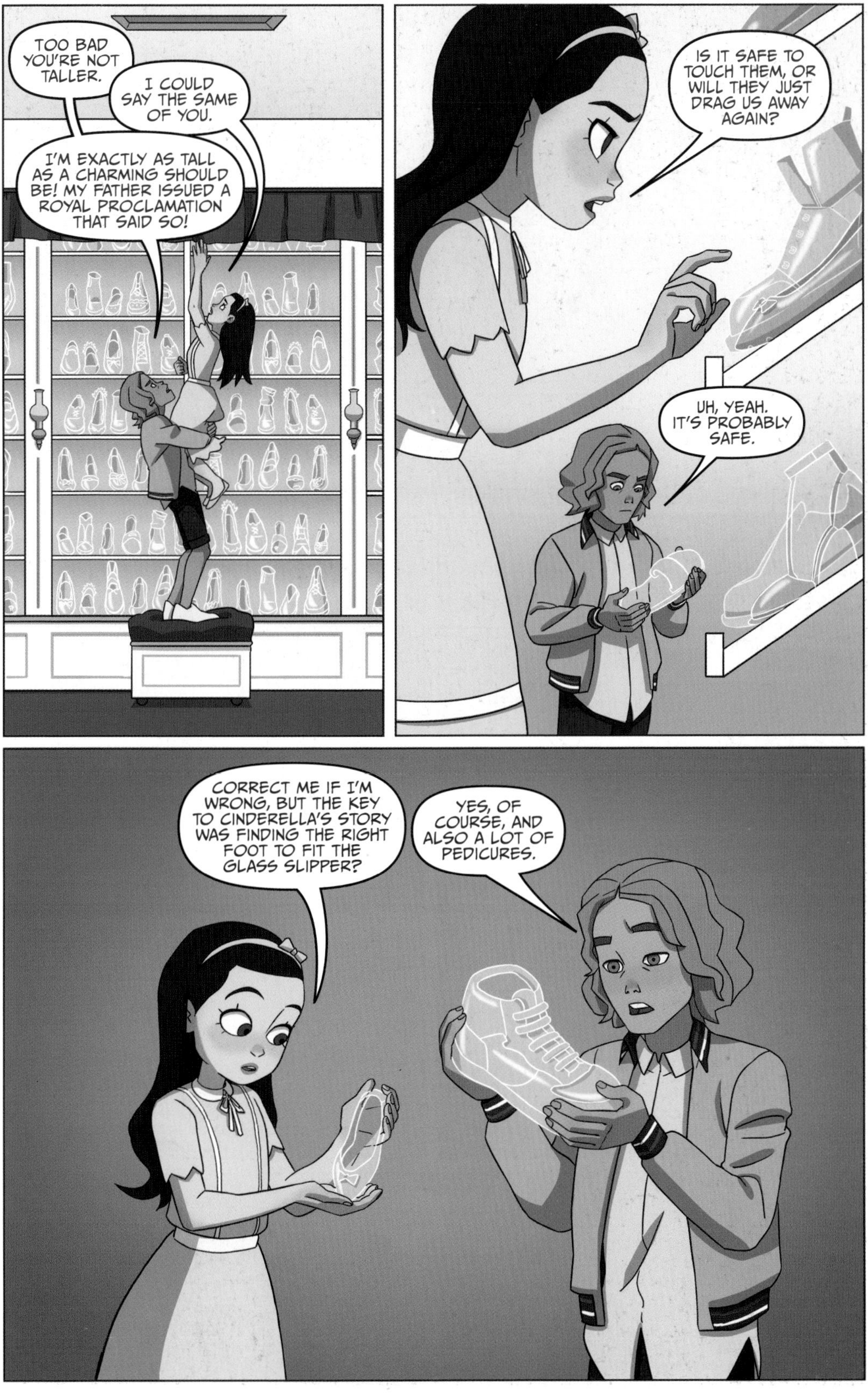
TOO BAD YOU'RE NOT TALLER.
I COULD SAY THE SAME OF YOU.
I'M EXACTLY AS TALL AS A CHARMING SHOULD BE! MY FATHER ISSUED A ROYAL PROCLAMATION THAT SAID SO!
IS IT SAFE TO TOUCH THEM, OR WILL THEY JUST DRAG US AWAY AGAIN?
UH, YEAH. IT'S PROBABLY SAFE.
CORRECT ME IF I'M WRONG, BUT THE KEY TO CINDERELLA'S STORY WAS FINDING THE RIGHT FOOT TO FIT THE GLASS SLIPPER?
YES, OF COURSE, AND ALSO A LOT OF PEDICURES.

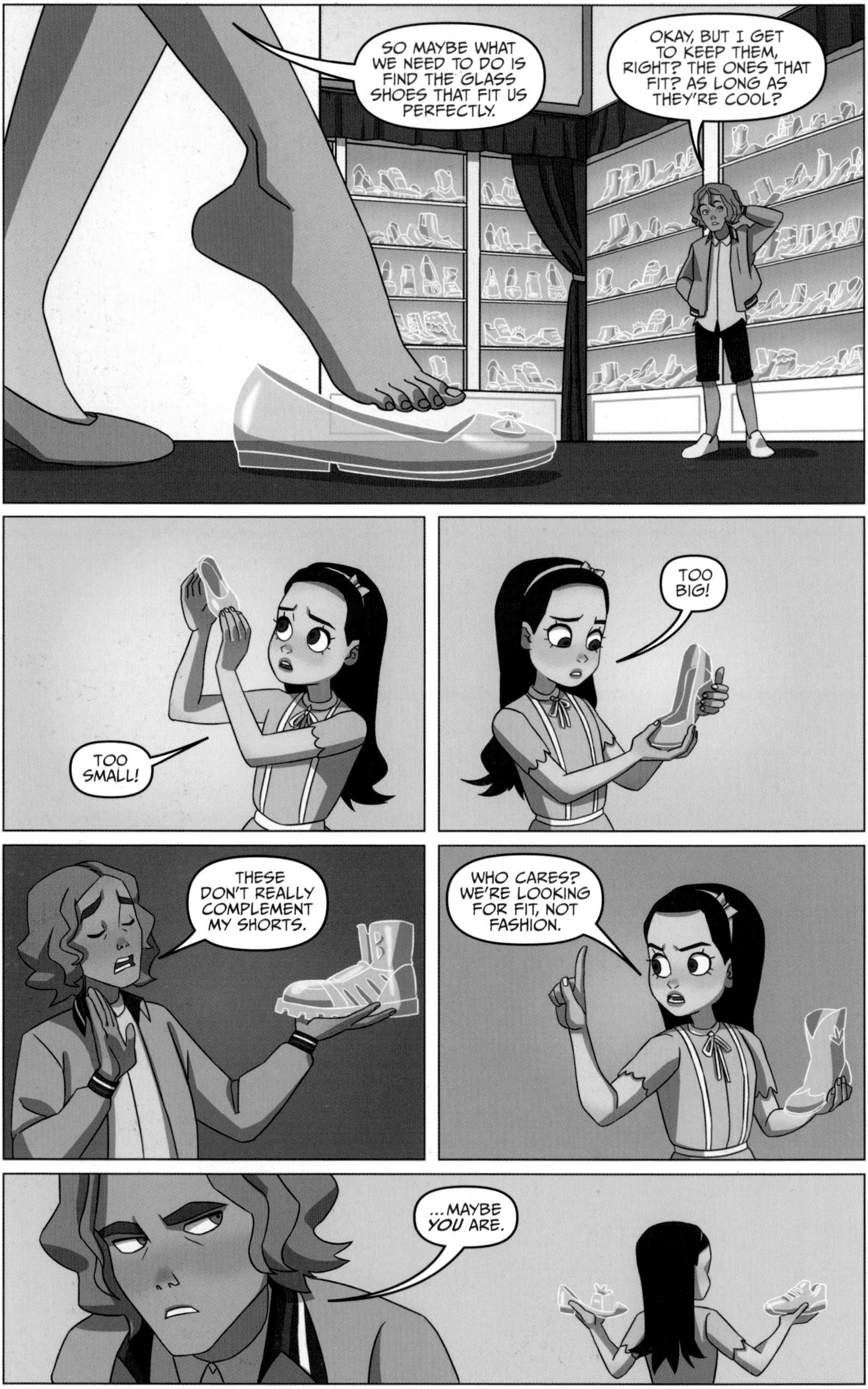
SO MAYBE WHAT WE NEED TO DO IS FIND THE GLASS SHOES THAT FIT US PERFECTLY.
OKAY, BUT I GET TO KEEP THEM, RIGHT? THE ONES THAT FIT? AS LONG AS THEY'RE COOL?
TOO SMALL!
TOO BIG!
THESE DON'T REALLY COMPLEMENT MY SHORTS.
WHO CARES? WE'RE LOOKING FOR FIT, NOT FASHION.
...MAYBE *YOU* ARE.

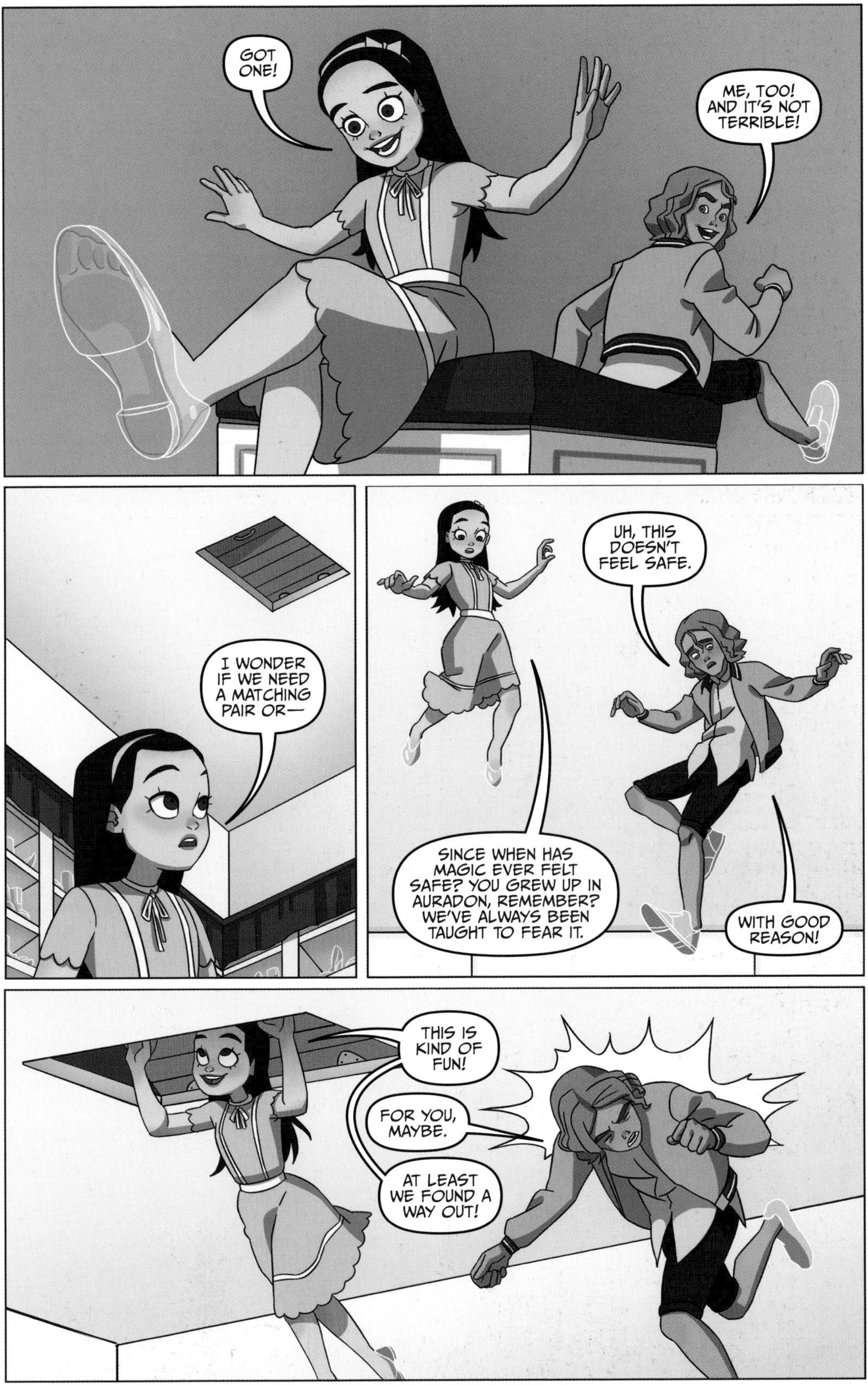
GOT ONE!
ME, TOO! AND IT'S NOT TERRIBLE!
I WONDER IF WE NEED A MATCHING PAIR OR—
UH, THIS DOESN'T FEEL SAFE.
SINCE WHEN HAS MAGIC EVER FELT SAFE? YOU GREW UP IN AURADON, REMEMBER? WE'VE ALWAYS BEEN TAUGHT TO FEAR IT.
WITH GOOD REASON!
THIS IS KIND OF FUN!
FOR YOU, MAYBE.
AT LEAST WE FOUND A WAY OUT!

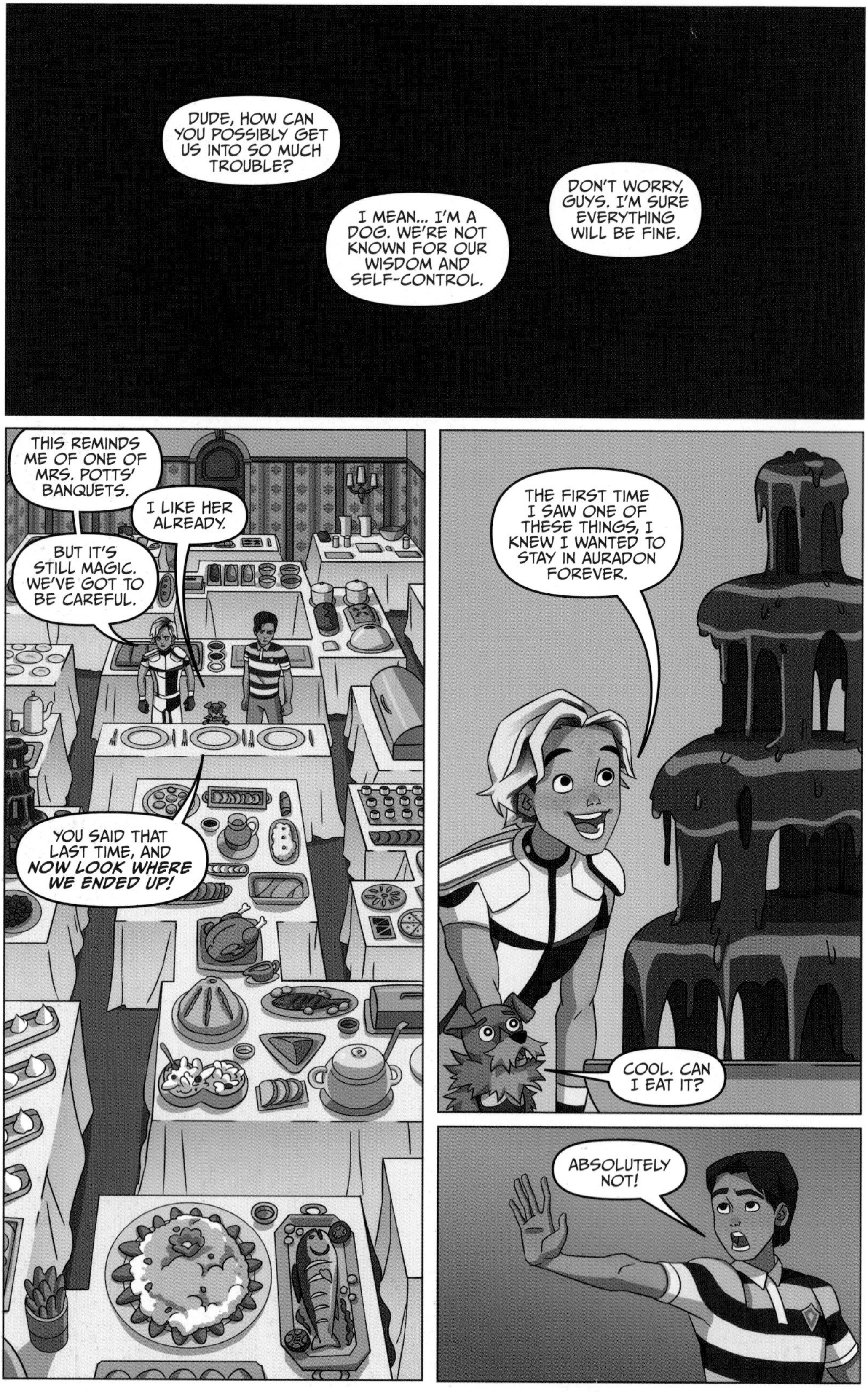
DUDE, HOW CAN YOU POSSIBLY GET US INTO SO MUCH TROUBLE?
I MEAN... I'M A DOG. WE'RE NOT KNOWN FOR OUR WISDOM AND SELF-CONTROL.
DON'T WORRY, GUYS. I'M SURE EVERYTHING WILL BE FINE.
THIS REMINDS ME OF ONE OF MRS. POTTS' BANQUETS.
I LIKE HER ALREADY.
BUT IT'S STILL MAGIC. WE'VE GOT TO BE CAREFUL.
YOU SAID THAT LAST TIME, AND *NOW LOOK WHERE WE ENDED UP!*
THE FIRST TIME I SAW ONE OF THESE THINGS, I KNEW I WANTED TO STAY IN AURADON FOREVER.
COOL. CAN I EAT IT?
ABSOLUTELY NOT!

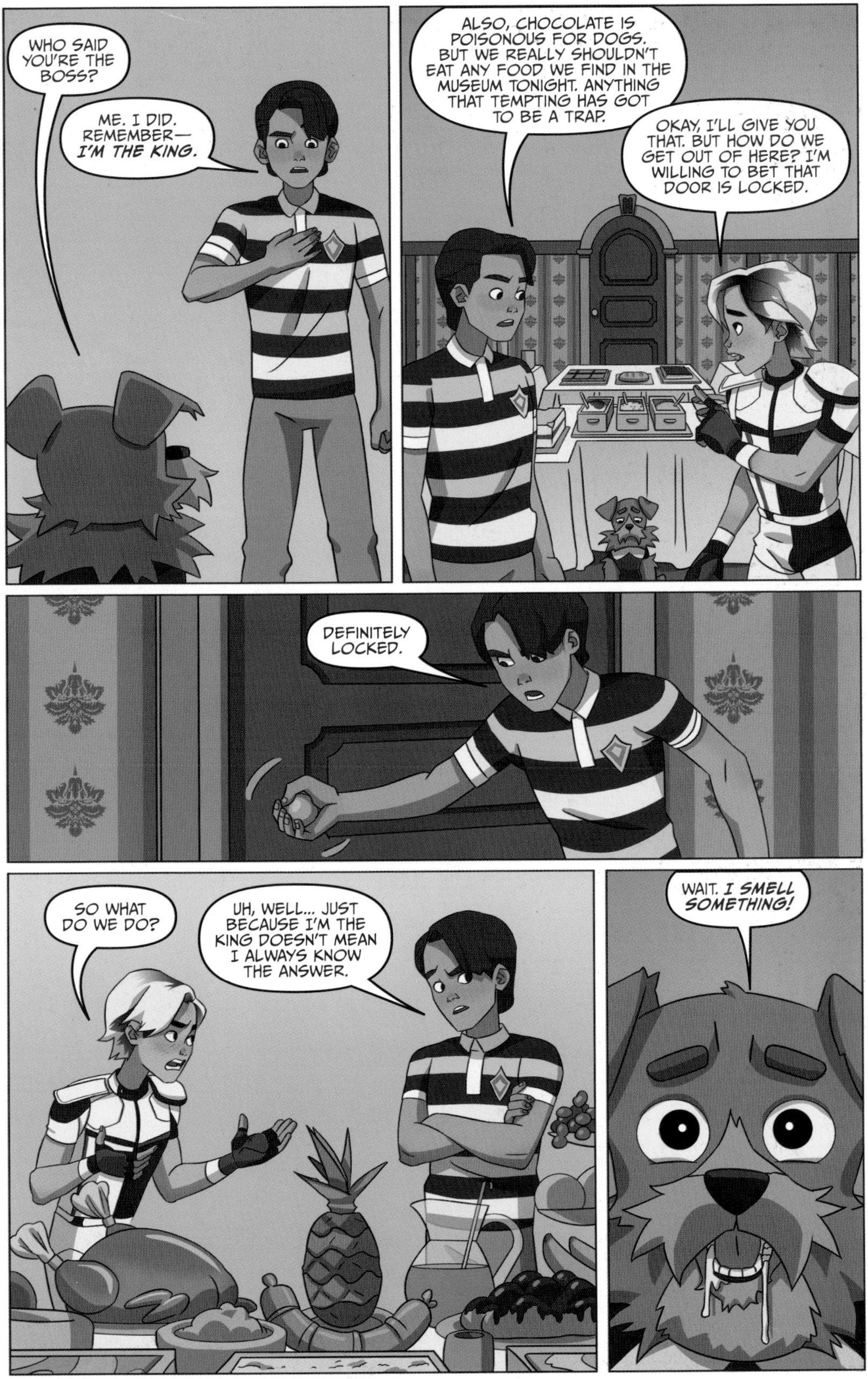
WHO SAID YOU'RE THE BOSS?
ME. I DID. REMEMBER— *I'M THE KING.*
ALSO, CHOCOLATE IS POISONOUS FOR DOGS. BUT WE REALLY SHOULDN'T EAT ANY FOOD WE FIND IN THE MUSEUM TONIGHT. ANYTHING THAT TEMPTING HAS GOT TO BE A TRAP.
OKAY, I'LL GIVE YOU THAT. BUT HOW DO WE GET OUT OF HERE? I'M WILLING TO BET THAT DOOR IS LOCKED.
DEFINITELY LOCKED.
SO WHAT DO WE DO?
UH, WELL... JUST BECAUSE I'M THE KING DOESN'T MEAN I ALWAYS KNOW THE ANSWER.
WAIT. *I SMELL SOMETHING!*

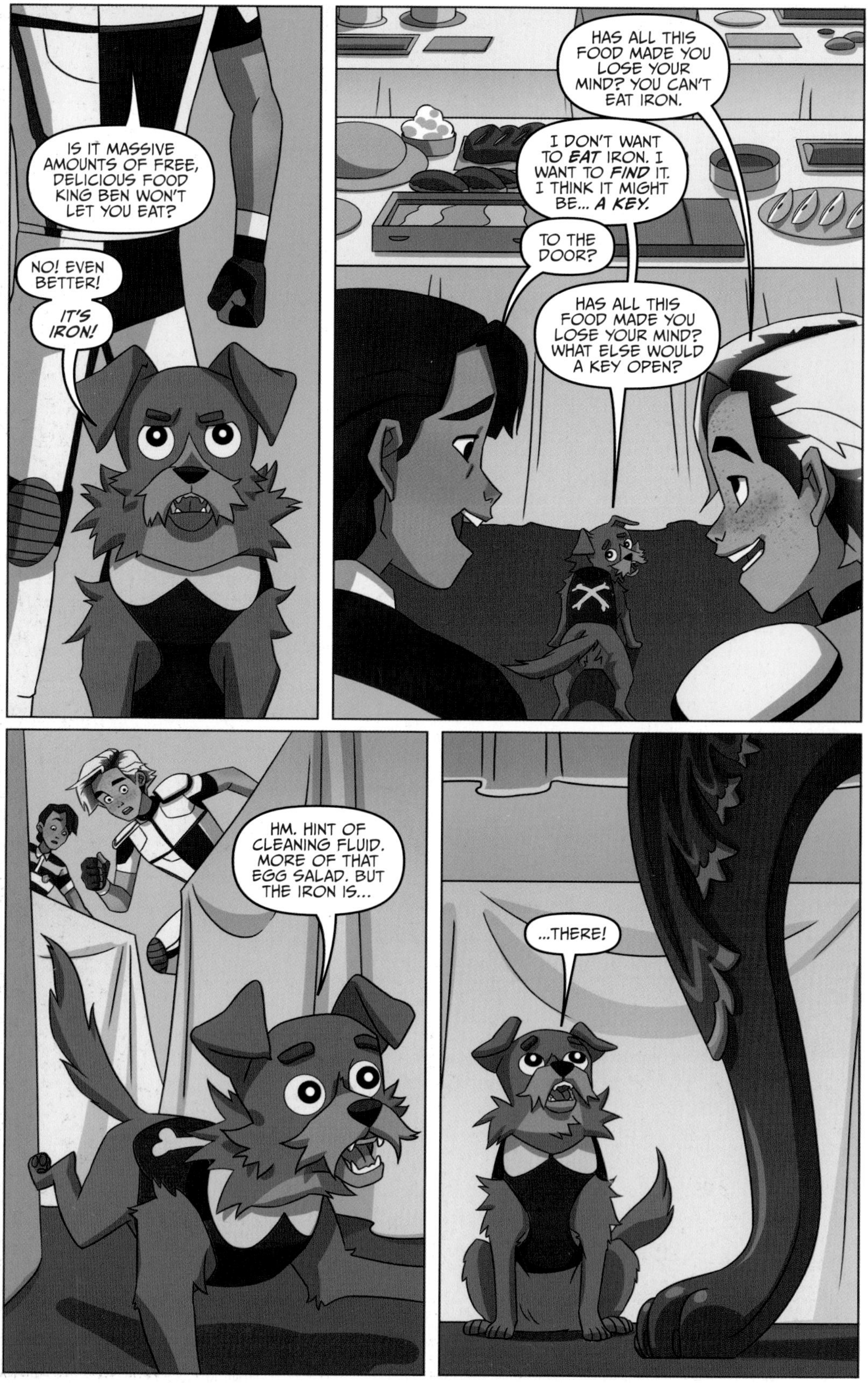
IS IT MASSIVE AMOUNTS OF FREE, DELICIOUS FOOD KING BEN WON'T LET YOU EAT?
NO! EVEN BETTER!
IT'S IRON!
HAS ALL THIS FOOD MADE YOU LOSE YOUR MIND? YOU CAN'T EAT IRON.
I DON'T WANT TO EAT IRON. I WANT TO FIND IT. I THINK IT MIGHT BE... A KEY.
TO THE DOOR?
HAS ALL THIS FOOD MADE YOU LOSE YOUR MIND? WHAT ELSE WOULD A KEY OPEN?
HM. HINT OF CLEANING FLUID. MORE OF THAT EGG SALAD. BUT THE IRON IS...
...THERE!

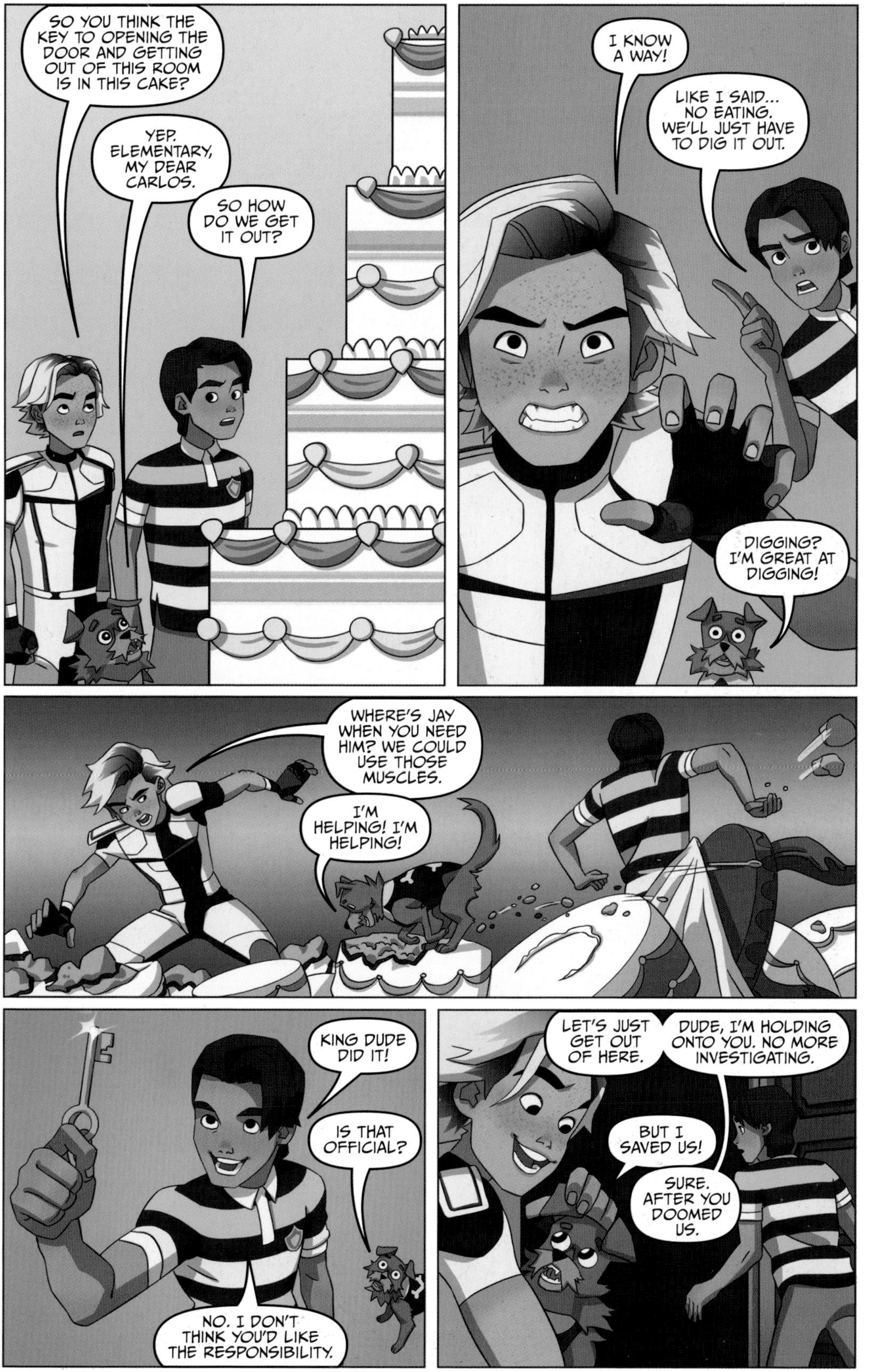
SO YOU THINK THE KEY TO OPENING THE DOOR AND GETTING OUT OF THIS ROOM IS IN THIS CAKE?
YEP. ELEMENTARY, MY DEAR CARLOS.
SO HOW DO WE GET IT OUT?
I KNOW A WAY!
LIKE I SAID... NO EATING. WE'LL JUST HAVE TO DIG IT OUT.
DIGGING? I'M GREAT AT DIGGING!
WHERE'S JAY WHEN YOU NEED HIM? WE COULD USE THOSE MUSCLES.
I'M HELPING! I'M HELPING!
KING DUDE DID IT!
IS THAT OFFICIAL?
NO. I DON'T THINK YOU'D LIKE THE RESPONSIBILITY.
LET'S JUST GET OUT OF HERE.
DUDE, I'M HOLDING ONTO YOU. NO MORE INVESTIGATING.
BUT I SAVED US!
SURE. AFTER YOU DOOMED US.

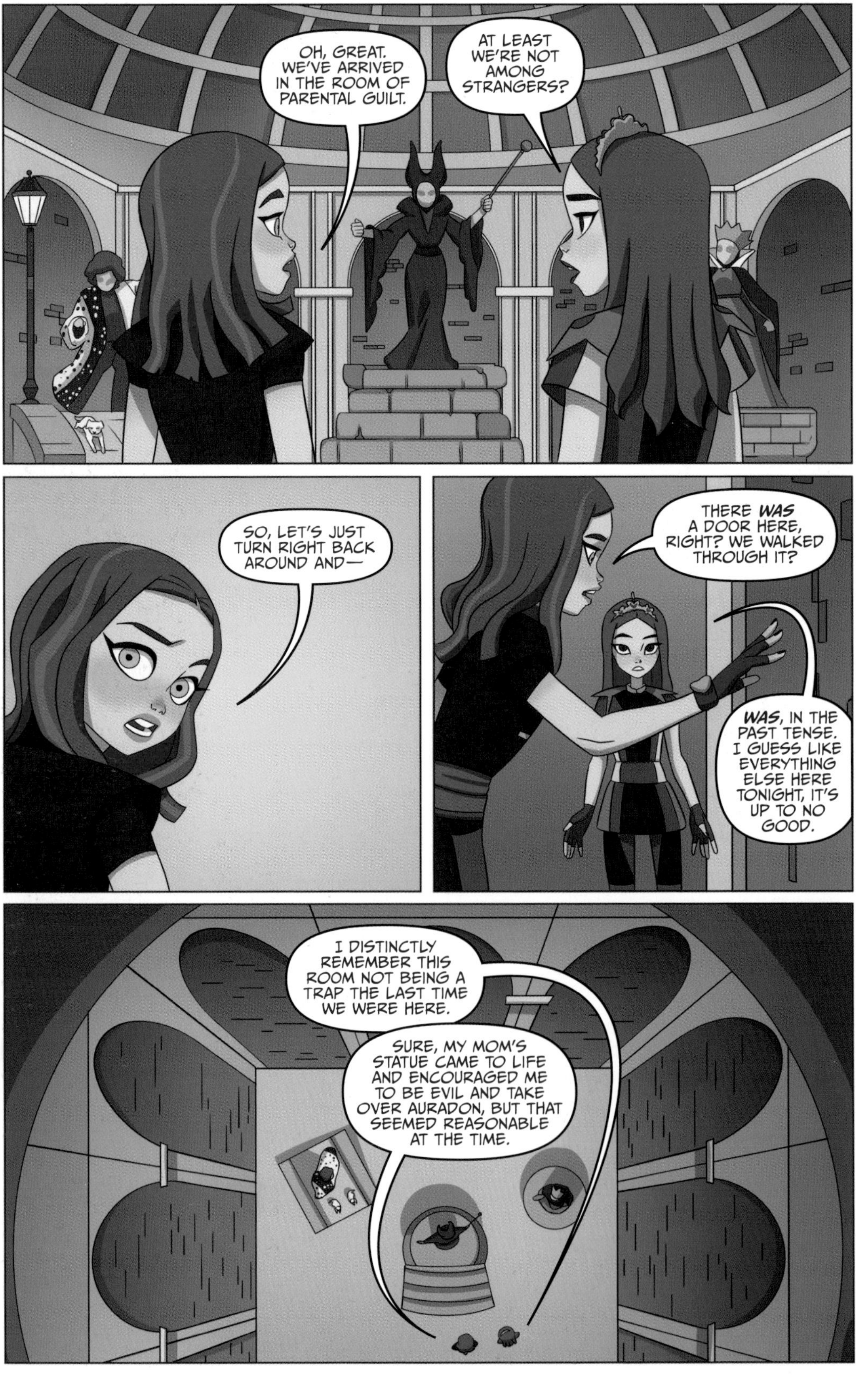
OH, GREAT. WE'VE ARRIVED IN THE ROOM OF PARENTAL GUILT.
AT LEAST WE'RE NOT AMONG STRANGERS?
SO, LET'S JUST TURN RIGHT BACK AROUND AND—
THERE *WAS* A DOOR HERE, RIGHT? WE WALKED THROUGH IT?
WAS, IN THE PAST TENSE. I GUESS LIKE EVERYTHING ELSE HERE TONIGHT, IT'S UP TO NO GOOD.
I DISTINCTLY REMEMBER THIS ROOM NOT BEING A TRAP THE LAST TIME WE WERE HERE.
SURE, MY MOM'S STATUE CAME TO LIFE AND ENCOURAGED ME TO BE EVIL AND TAKE OVER AURADON, BUT THAT SEEMED REASONABLE AT THE TIME.

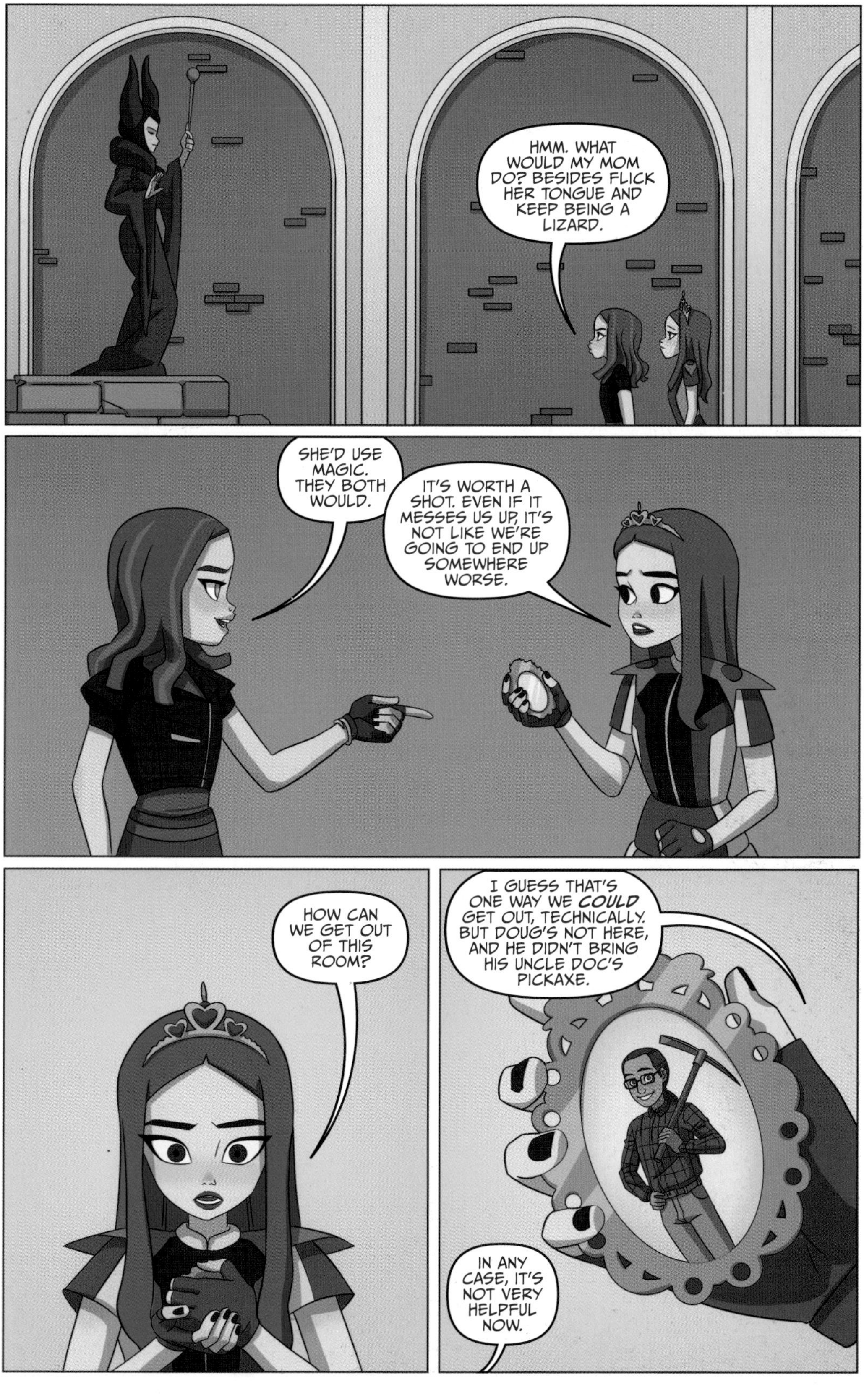
HMM. WHAT WOULD MY MOM DO? BESIDES FLICK HER TONGUE AND KEEP BEING A LIZARD.
SHE'D USE MAGIC. THEY BOTH WOULD.
IT'S WORTH A SHOT. EVEN IF IT MESSES US UP, IT'S NOT LIKE WE'RE GOING TO END UP SOMEWHERE WORSE.
HOW CAN WE GET OUT OF THIS ROOM?
I GUESS THAT'S ONE WAY WE *COULD* GET OUT, TECHNICALLY. BUT DOUG'S NOT HERE, AND HE DIDN'T BRING HIS UNCLE DOC'S PICKAXE.
IN ANY CASE, IT'S NOT VERY HELPFUL NOW.

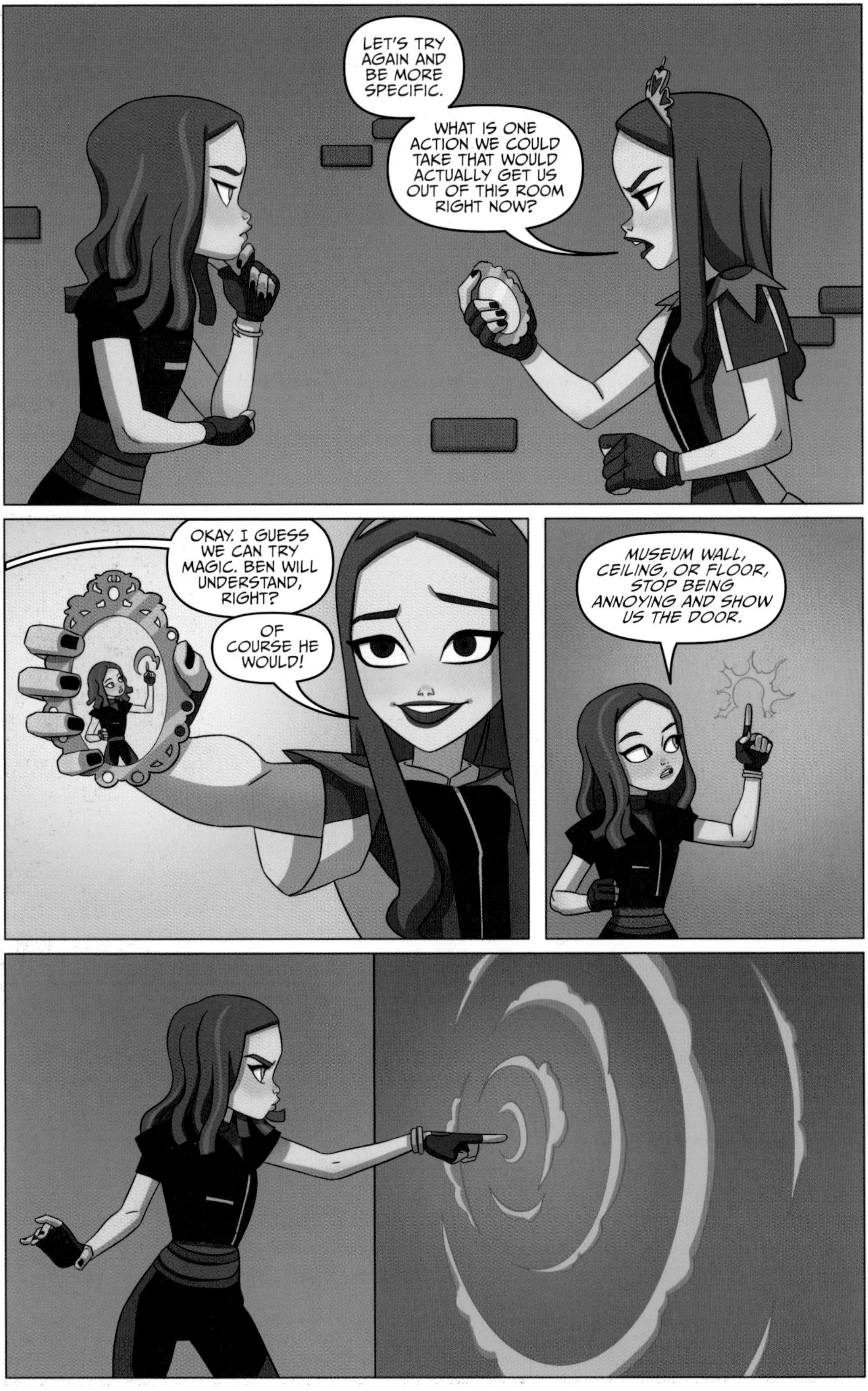
LET'S TRY AGAIN AND BE MORE SPECIFIC.
WHAT IS ONE ACTION WE COULD TAKE THAT WOULD ACTUALLY GET US OUT OF THIS ROOM RIGHT NOW?
OKAY. I GUESS WE CAN TRY MAGIC. BEN WILL UNDERSTAND, RIGHT?
OF COURSE HE WOULD!
MUSEUM WALL, CEILING, OR FLOOR, STOP BEING ANNOYING AND SHOW US THE DOOR.

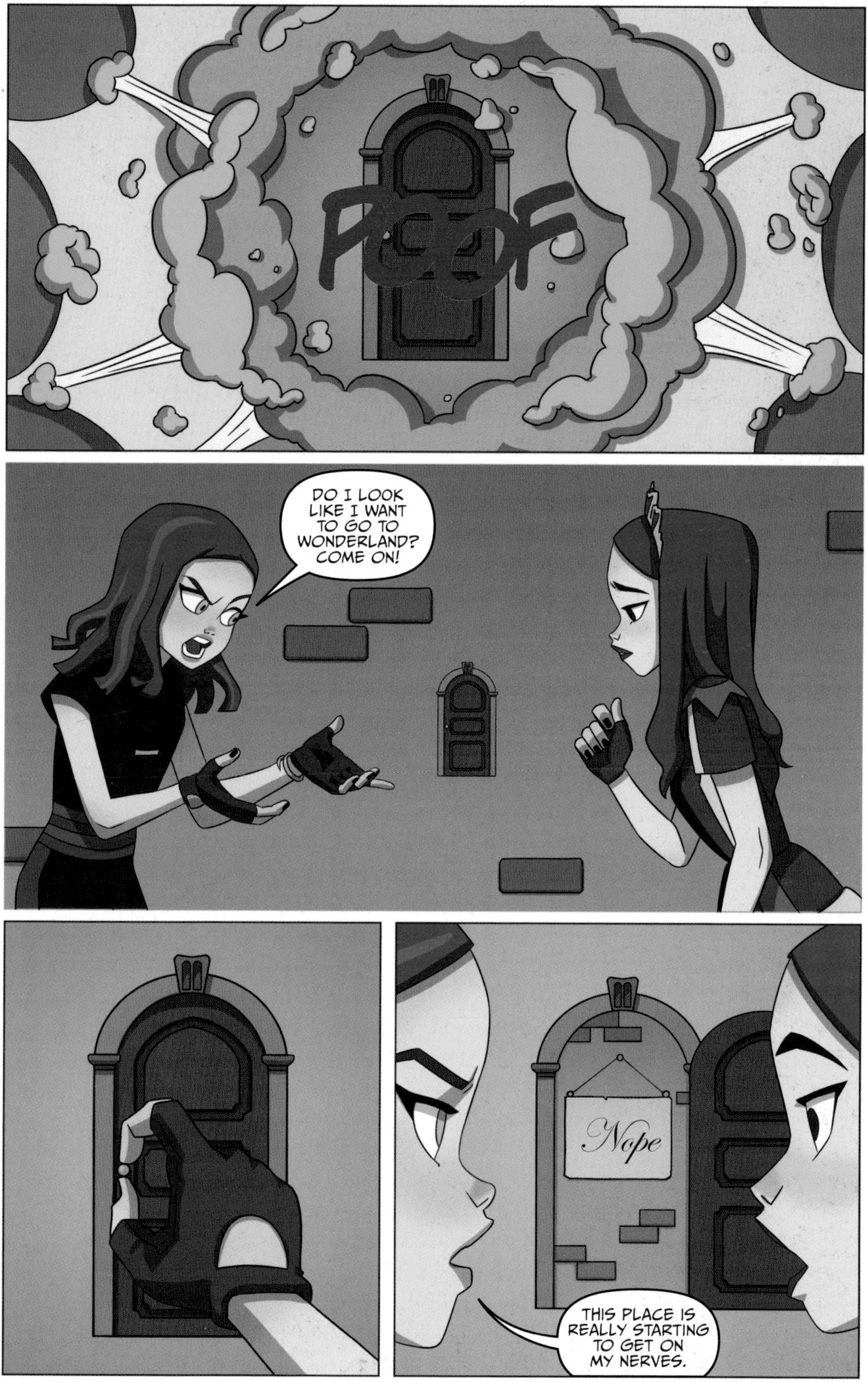
POOF
DO I LOOK LIKE I WANT TO GO TO WONDERLAND? COME ON!
Nope
THIS PLACE IS REALLY STARTING TO GET ON MY NERVES.

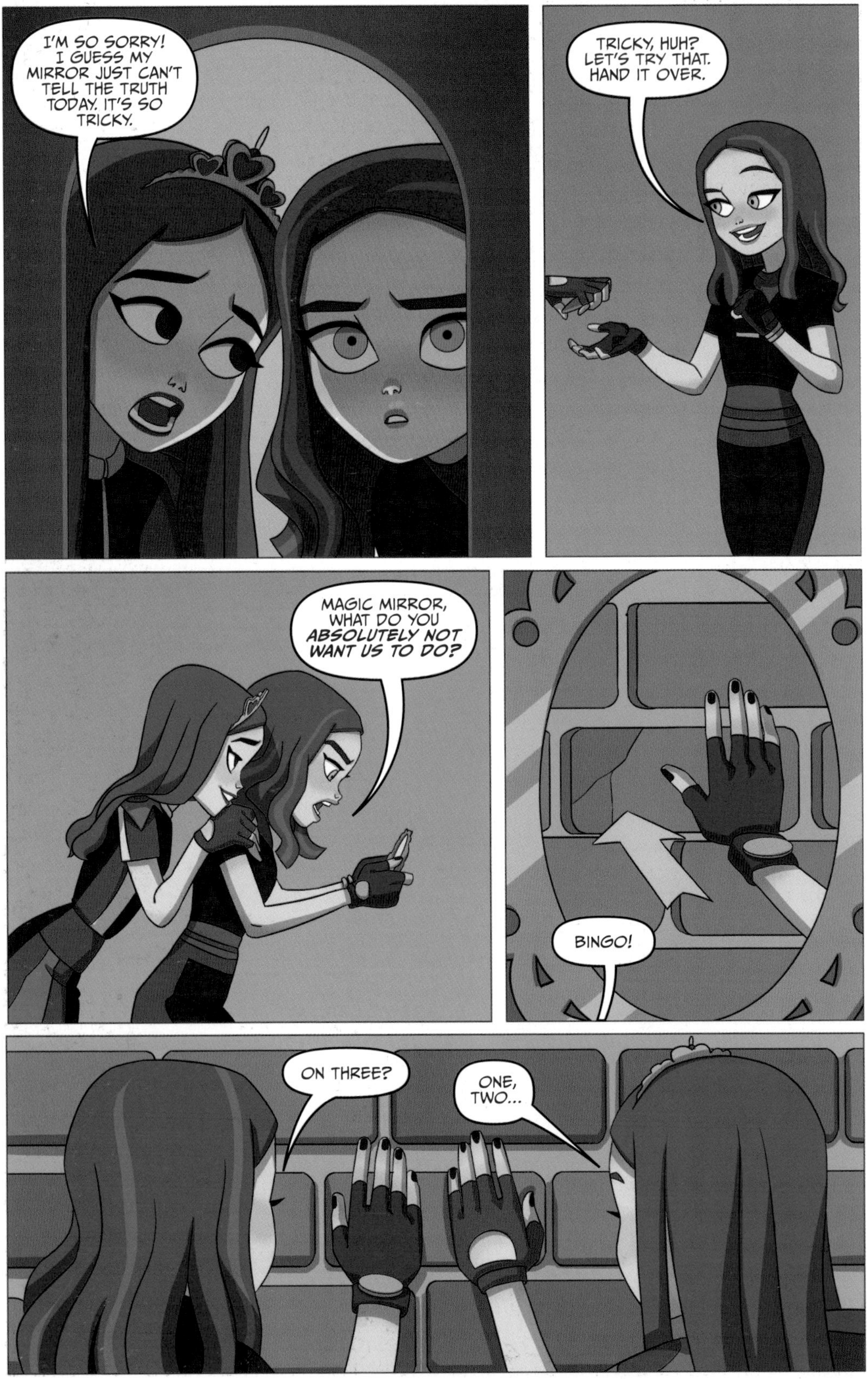
I'M SO SORRY! I GUESS MY MIRROR JUST CAN'T TELL THE TRUTH TODAY. IT'S SO TRICKY.
TRICKY, HUH? LET'S TRY THAT. HAND IT OVER.
MAGIC MIRROR, WHAT DO YOU *ABSOLUTELY NOT WANT US TO DO?*
BINGO!
ON THREE?
ONE, TWO...

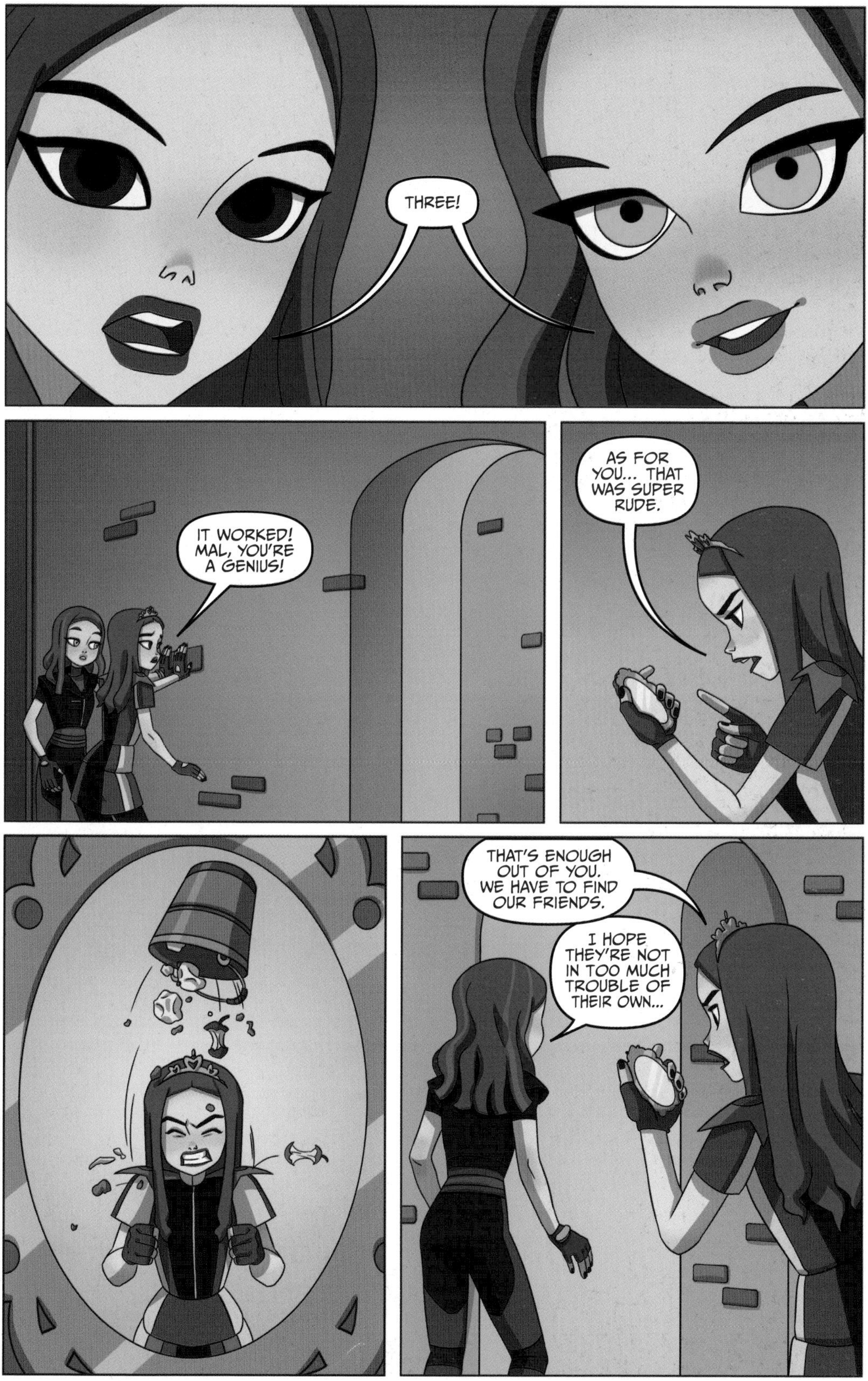
THREE!
IT WORKED! MAL, YOU'RE A GENIUS!
AS FOR YOU... THAT WAS SUPER RUDE.
THAT'S ENOUGH OUT OF YOU. WE HAVE TO FIND OUR FRIENDS.
I HOPE THEY'RE NOT IN TOO MUCH TROUBLE OF THEIR OWN...

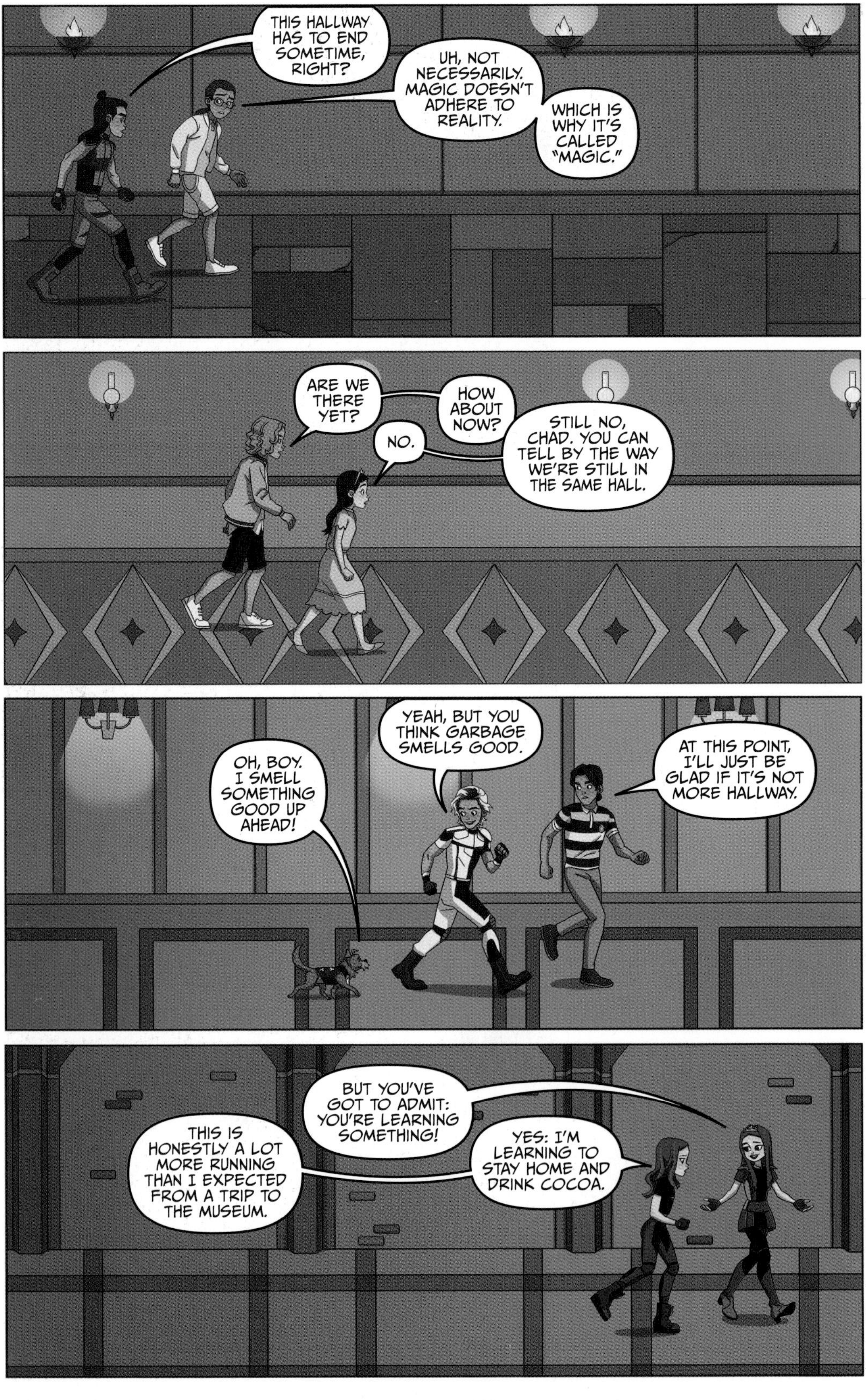
THIS HALLWAY HAS TO END SOMETIME, RIGHT?
UH, NOT NECESSARILY. MAGIC DOESN'T ADHERE TO REALITY.
WHICH IS WHY IT'S CALLED "MAGIC."
ARE WE THERE YET?
NO.
HOW ABOUT NOW?
STILL NO, CHAD. YOU CAN TELL BY THE WAY WE'RE STILL IN THE SAME HALL.
OH, BOY. I SMELL SOMETHING GOOD UP AHEAD!
YEAH, BUT YOU THINK GARBAGE SMELLS GOOD.
AT THIS POINT, I'LL JUST BE GLAD IF IT'S NOT MORE HALLWAY.
THIS IS HONESTLY A LOT MORE RUNNING THAN I EXPECTED FROM A TRIP TO THE MUSEUM.
BUT YOU'VE GOT TO ADMIT: YOU'RE LEARNING SOMETHING!
YES: I'M LEARNING TO STAY HOME AND DRINK COCOA.

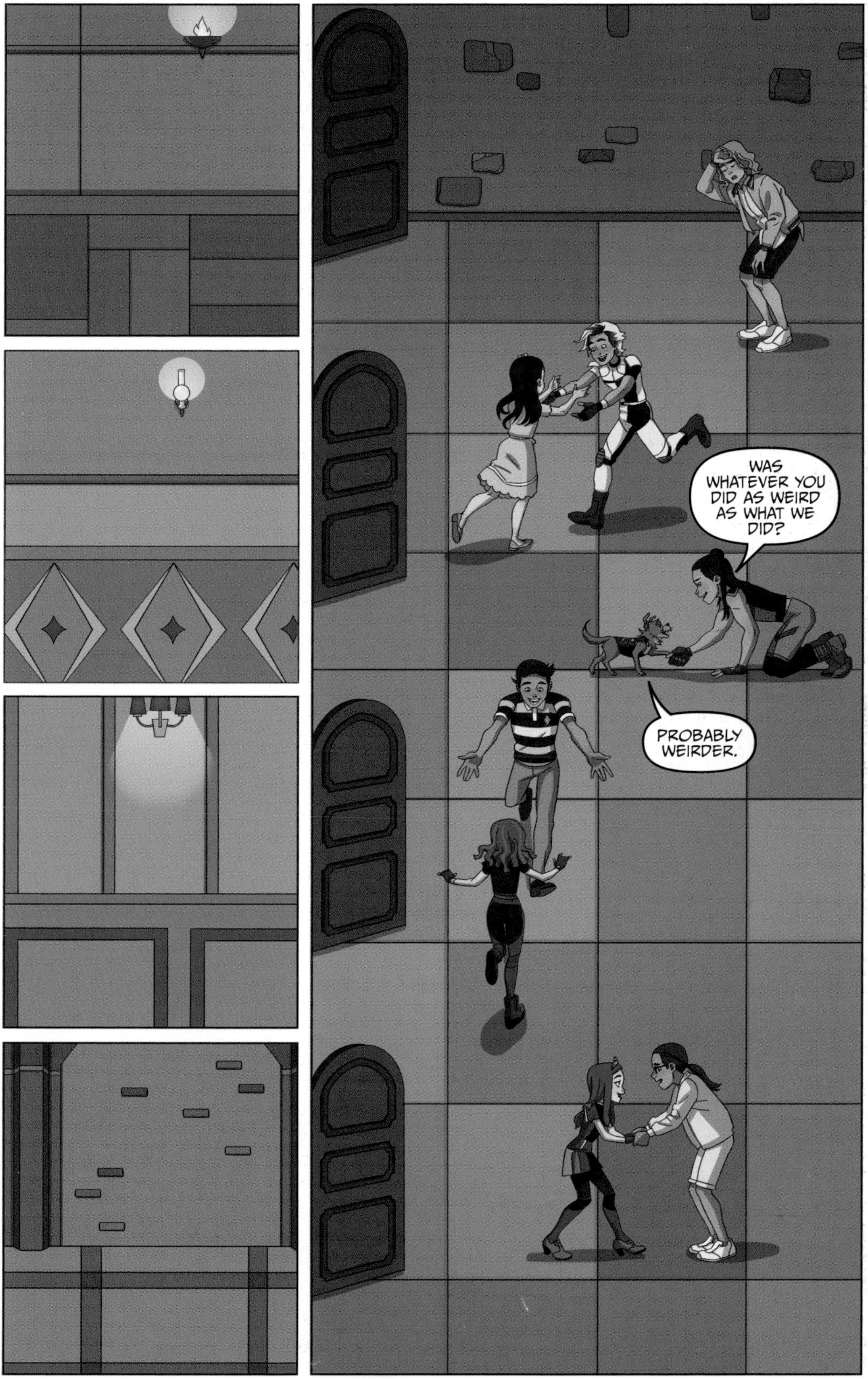
WAS WHATEVER YOU DID AS WEIRD AS WHAT WE DID?
PROBABLY WEIRDER.

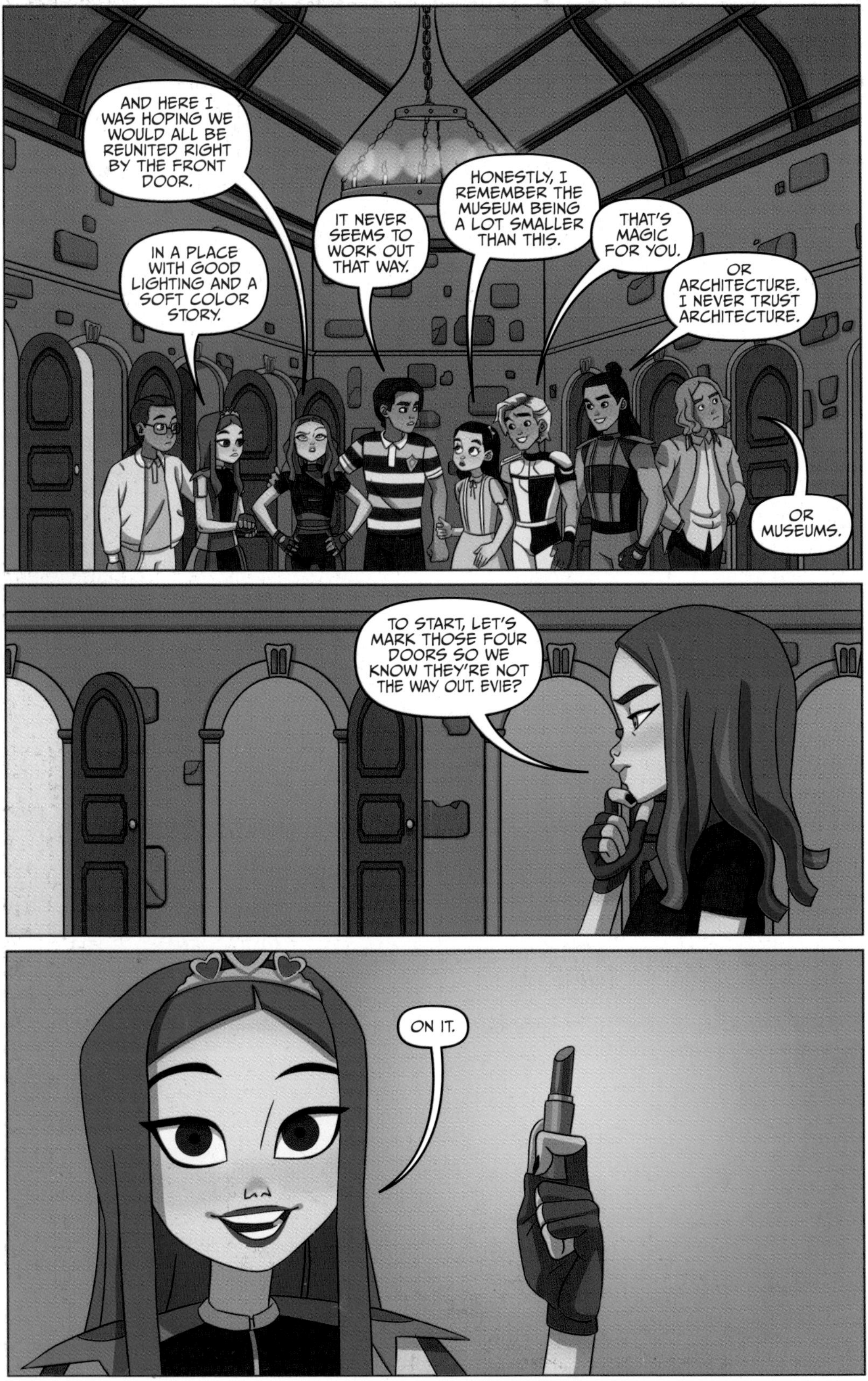
AND HERE I WAS HOPING WE WOULD ALL BE REUNITED RIGHT BY THE FRONT DOOR.
IN A PLACE WITH GOOD LIGHTING AND A SOFT COLOR STORY.
IT NEVER SEEMS TO WORK OUT THAT WAY.
HONESTLY, I REMEMBER THE MUSEUM BEING A LOT SMALLER THAN THIS.
THAT'S MAGIC FOR YOU.
OR ARCHITECTURE. I NEVER TRUST ARCHITECTURE.
OR MUSEUMS.
TO START, LET'S MARK THOSE FOUR DOORS SO WE KNOW THEY'RE NOT THE WAY OUT. EVIE?
ON IT.

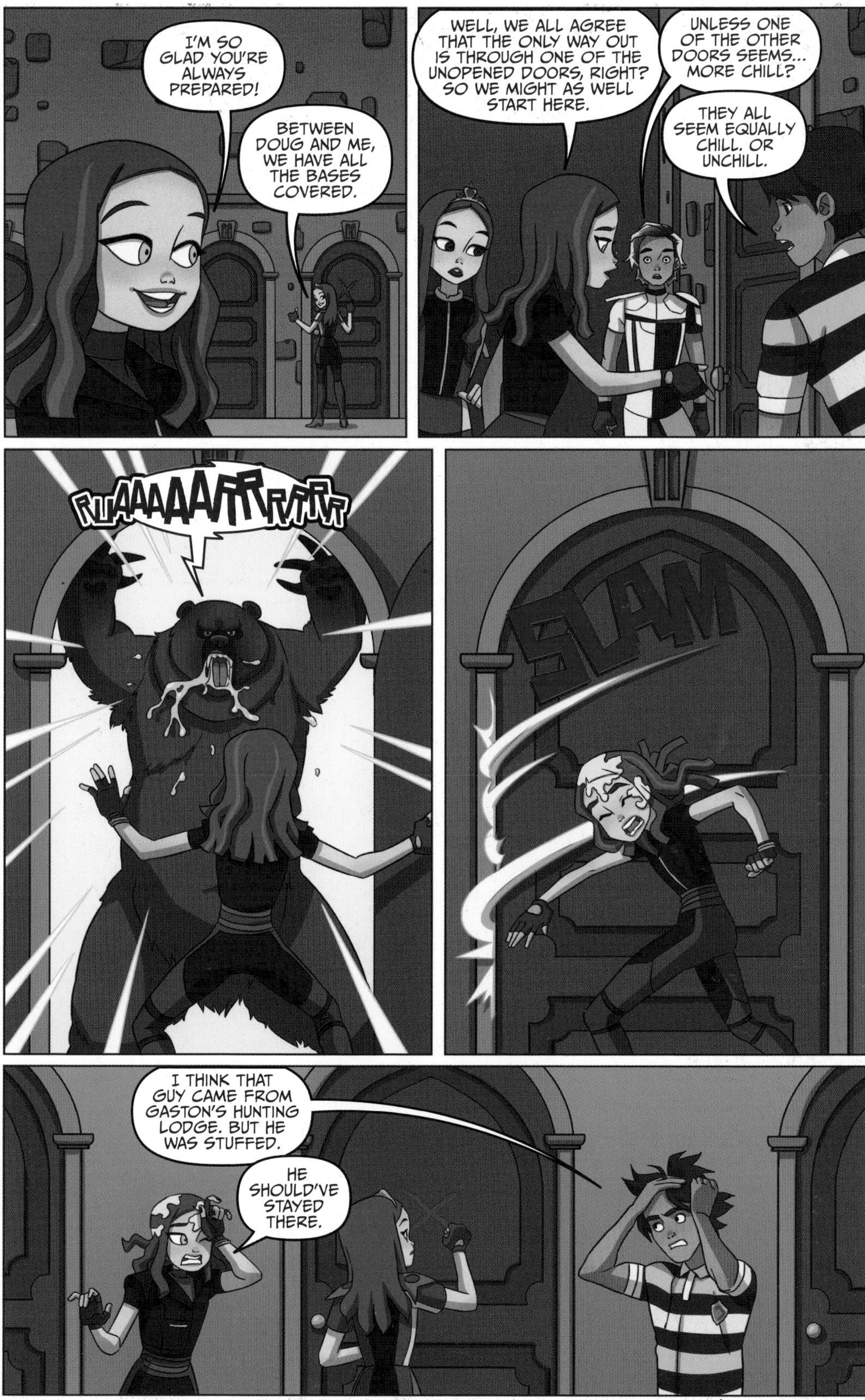
I'M SO GLAD YOU'RE ALWAYS PREPARED!
BETWEEN DOUG AND ME, WE HAVE ALL THE BASES COVERED.
WELL, WE ALL AGREE THAT THE ONLY WAY OUT IS THROUGH ONE OF THE UNOPENED DOORS, RIGHT? SO WE MIGHT AS WELL START HERE.
UNLESS ONE OF THE OTHER DOORS SEEMS... MORE CHILL?
THEY ALL SEEM EQUALLY CHILL. OR UNCHILL.
RUAAAAARRRRRRR
SLAM
I THINK THAT GUY CAME FROM GASTON'S HUNTING LODGE. BUT HE WAS STUFFED.
HE SHOULD'VE STAYED THERE.

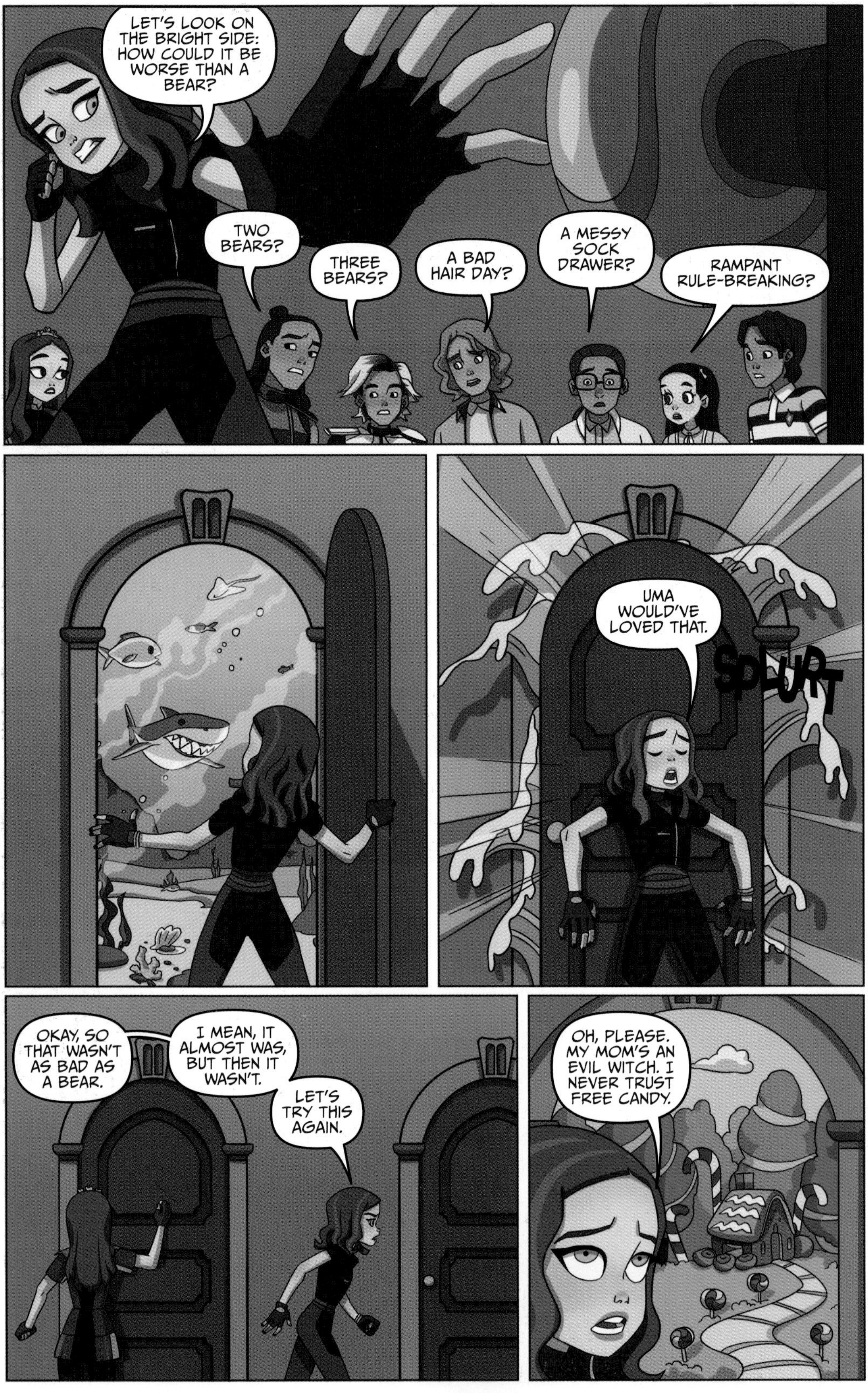
LET'S LOOK ON THE BRIGHT SIDE: HOW COULD IT BE WORSE THAN A BEAR?
TWO BEARS?
THREE BEARS?
A BAD HAIR DAY?
A MESSY SOCK DRAWER?
RAMPANT RULE-BREAKING?
UMA WOULD'VE LOVED THAT.
SPLURT
OKAY, SO THAT WASN'T AS BAD AS A BEAR.
I MEAN, IT ALMOST WAS, BUT THEN IT WASN'T.
LET'S TRY THIS AGAIN.
OH, PLEASE. MY MOM'S AN EVIL WITCH. I NEVER TRUST FREE CANDY.

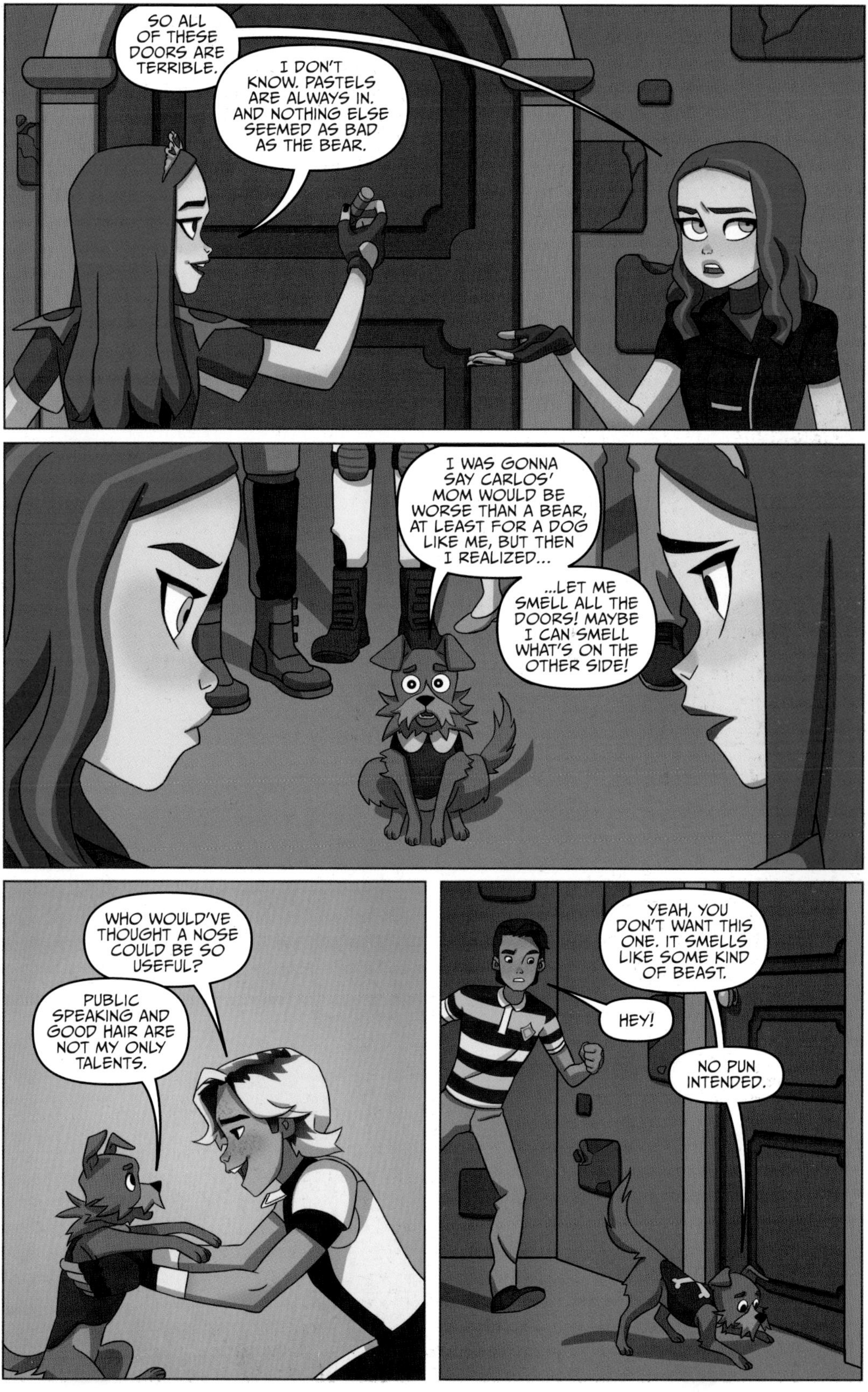
SO ALL OF THESE DOORS ARE TERRIBLE.
I DON'T KNOW. PASTELS ARE ALWAYS IN. AND NOTHING ELSE SEEMED AS BAD AS THE BEAR.
I WAS GONNA SAY CARLOS' MOM WOULD BE WORSE THAN A BEAR, AT LEAST FOR A DOG LIKE ME, BUT THEN I REALIZED...
...LET ME SMELL ALL THE DOORS! MAYBE I CAN SMELL WHAT'S ON THE OTHER SIDE!
WHO WOULD'VE THOUGHT A NOSE COULD BE SO USEFUL?
PUBLIC SPEAKING AND GOOD HAIR ARE NOT MY ONLY TALENTS.
YEAH, YOU DON'T WANT THIS ONE. IT SMELLS LIKE SOME KIND OF BEAST.
HEY!
NO PUN INTENDED.

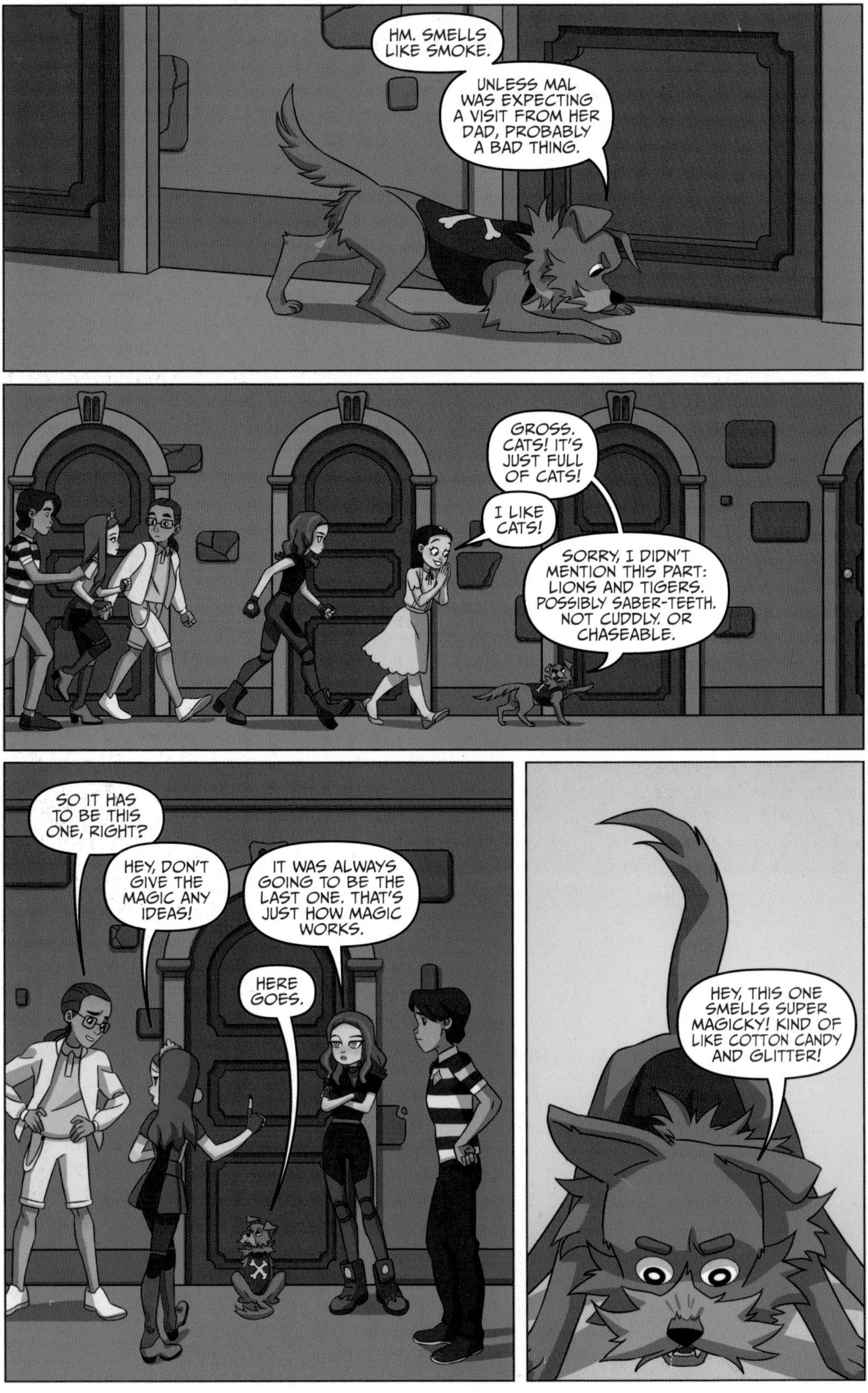
HM. SMELLS LIKE SMOKE.
UNLESS MAL WAS EXPECTING A VISIT FROM HER DAD, PROBABLY A BAD THING.
GROSS. CATS! IT'S JUST FULL OF CATS!
I LIKE CATS!
SORRY, I DIDN'T MENTION THIS PART: LIONS AND TIGERS. POSSIBLY SABER-TEETH. NOT CUDDLY. OR CHASEABLE.
SO IT HAS TO BE THIS ONE, RIGHT?
HEY, DON'T GIVE THE MAGIC ANY IDEAS!
IT WAS ALWAYS GOING TO BE THE LAST ONE. THAT'S JUST HOW MAGIC WORKS.
HERE GOES.
HEY, THIS ONE SMELLS SUPER MAGICKY! KIND OF LIKE COTTON CANDY AND GLITTER!

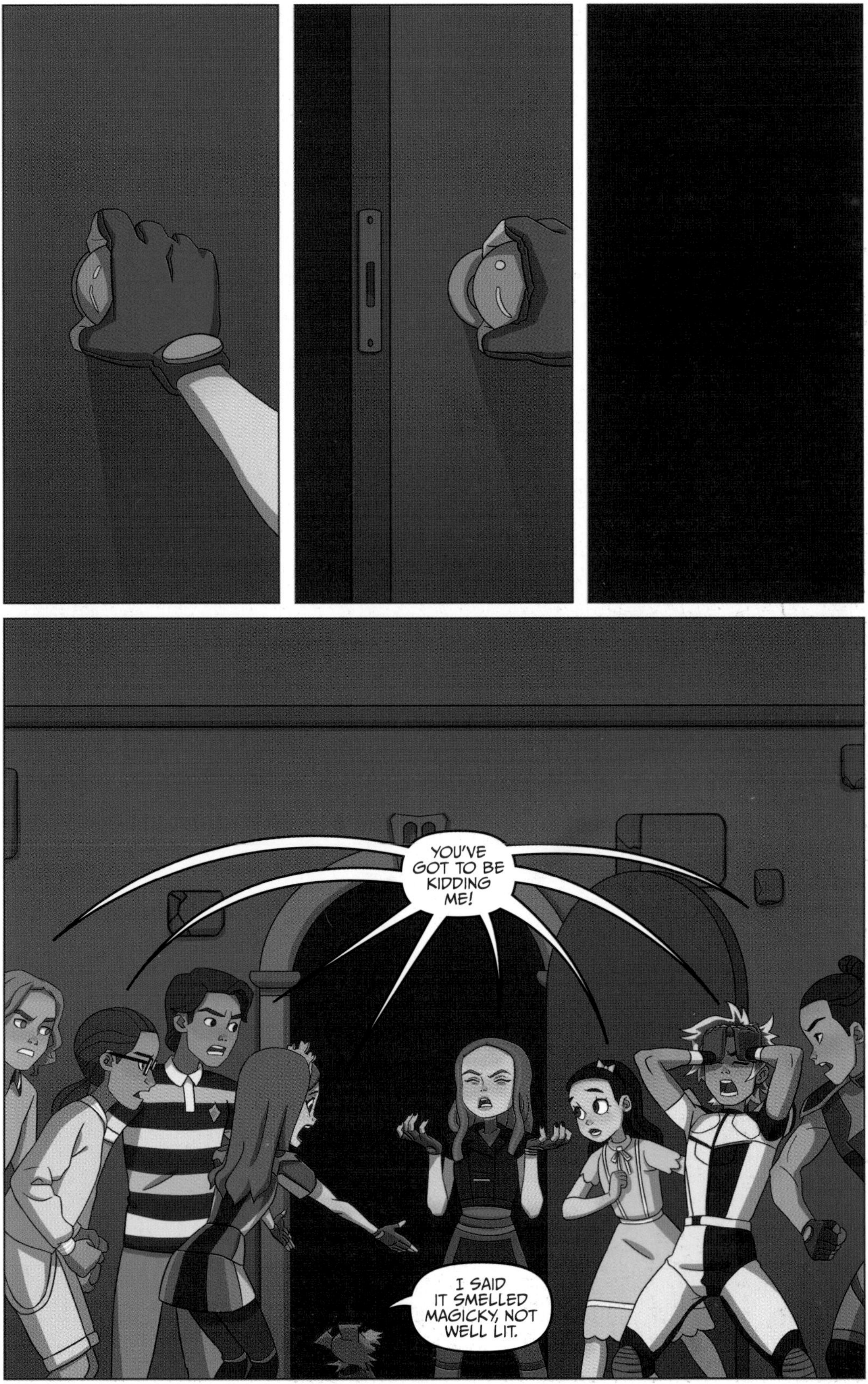
YOU'VE GOT TO BE KIDDING ME!
I SAID IT SMELLED MAGICKY, NOT WELL LIT.

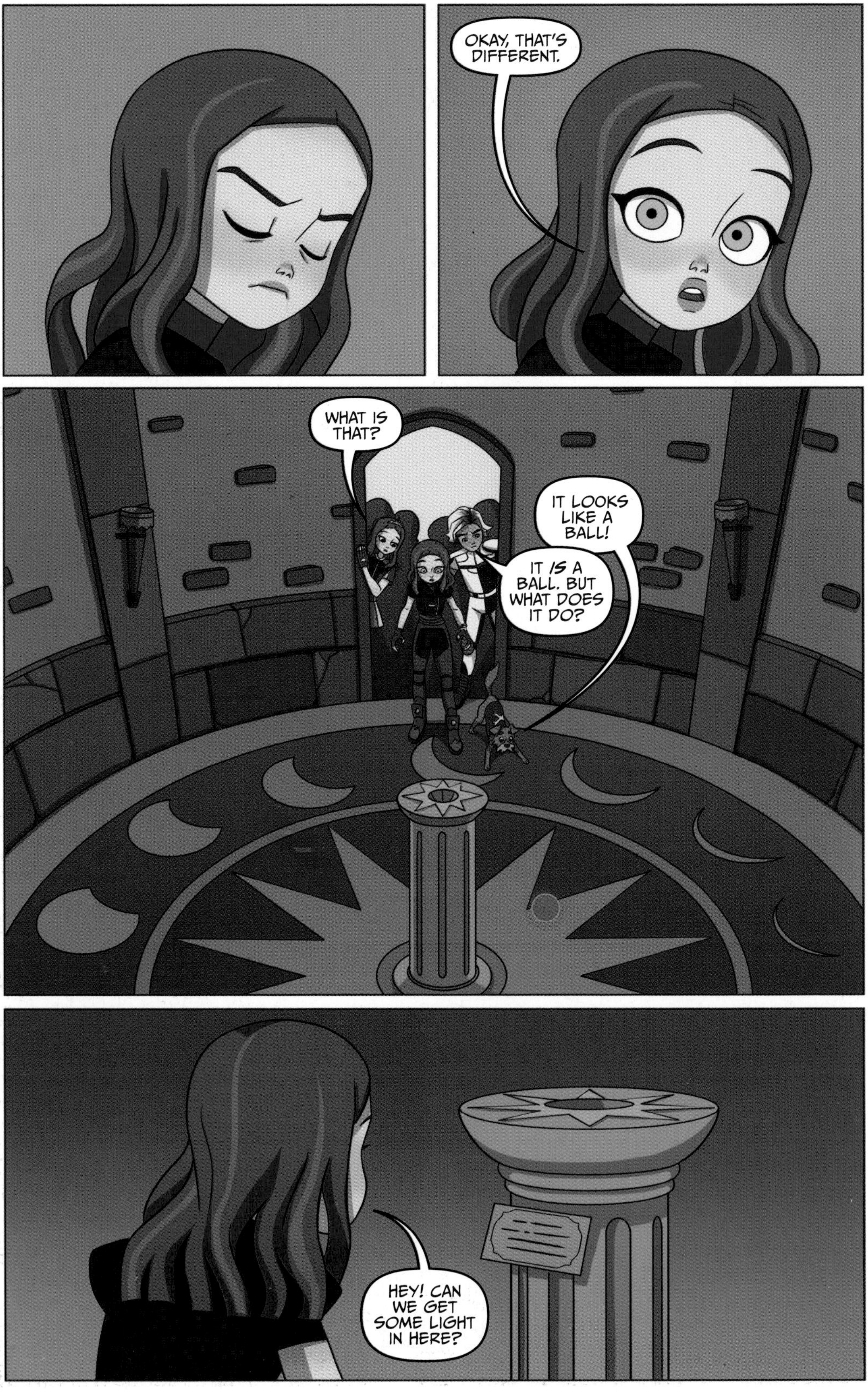
OKAY, THAT'S DIFFERENT.
WHAT IS THAT?
IT LOOKS LIKE A BALL!
IT *IS* A BALL. BUT WHAT DOES IT DO?
HEY! CAN WE GET SOME LIGHT IN HERE?

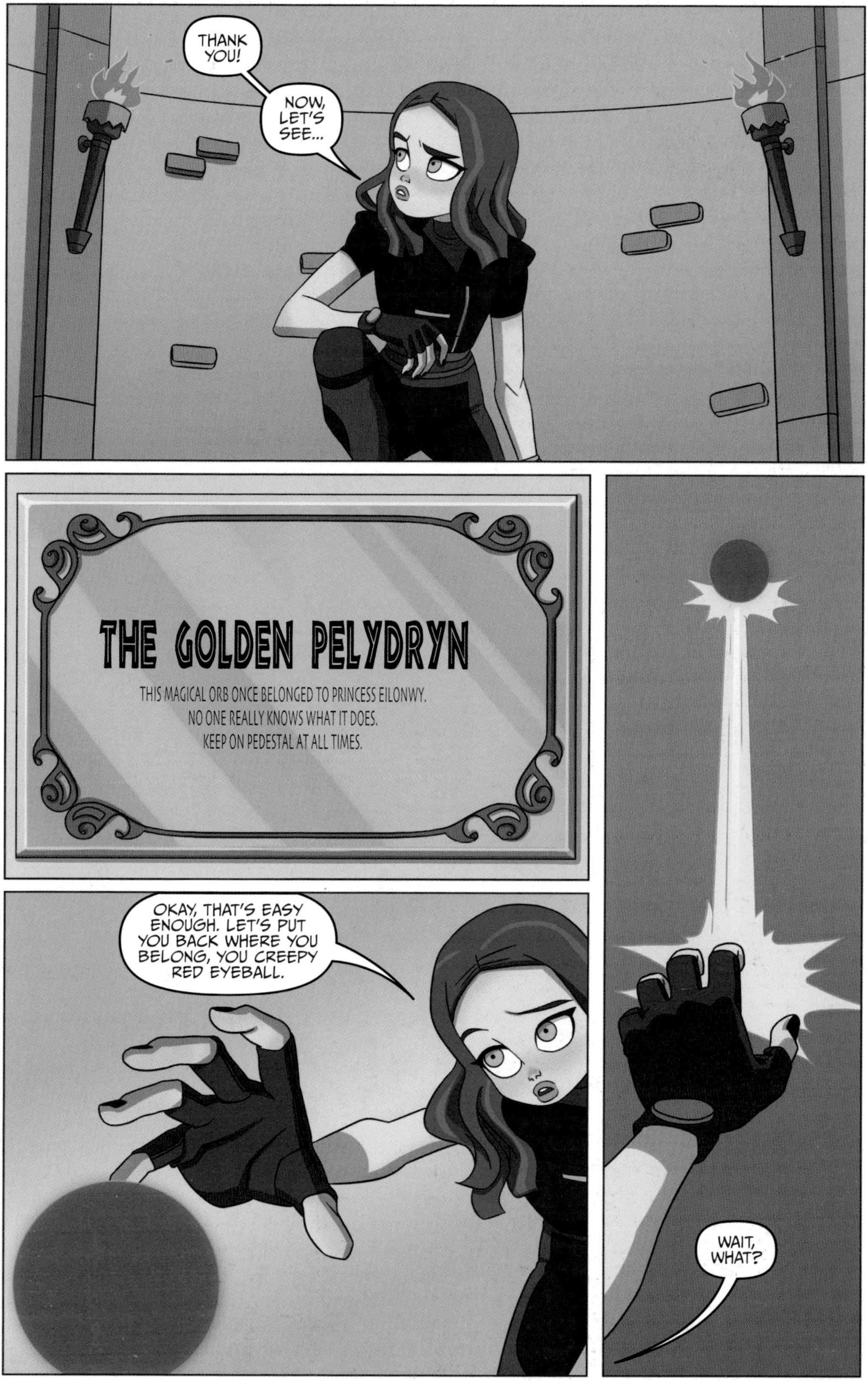
THANK YOU!
NOW, LET'S SEE...
THE GOLDEN PELYDRYN
THIS MAGICAL ORB ONCE BELONGED TO PRINCESS EILONWY.
NO ONE REALLY KNOWS WHAT IT DOES.
KEEP ON PEDESTAL AT ALL TIMES.
OKAY, THAT'S EASY ENOUGH. LET'S PUT YOU BACK WHERE YOU BELONG, YOU CREEPY RED EYEBALL.
WAIT, WHAT?

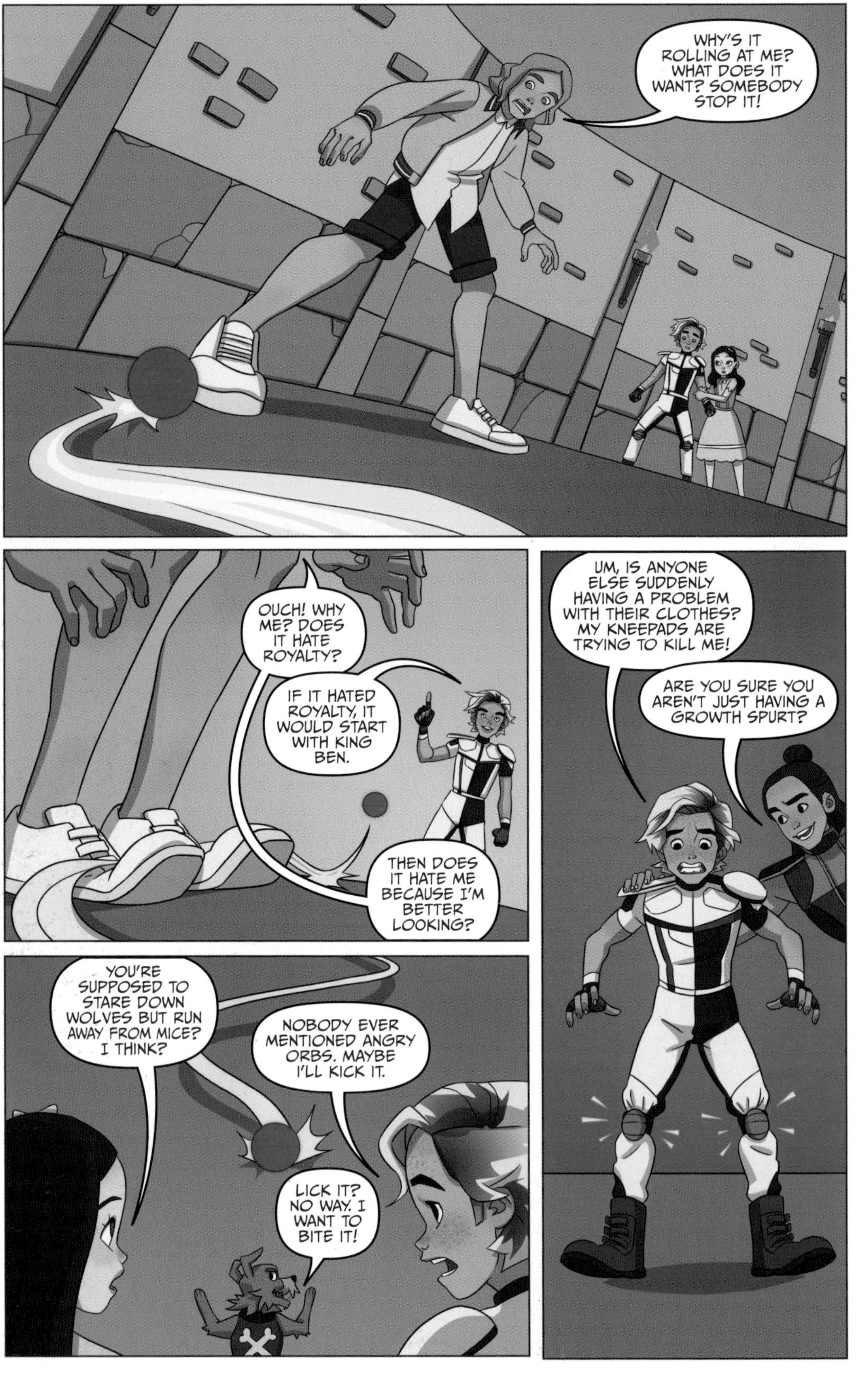
WHY'S IT ROLLING AT ME? WHAT DOES IT WANT? SOMEBODY STOP IT!
OUCH! WHY ME? DOES IT HATE ROYALTY?
IF IT HATED ROYALTY, IT WOULD START WITH KING BEN.
THEN DOES IT HATE ME BECAUSE I'M BETTER LOOKING?
YOU'RE SUPPOSED TO STARE DOWN WOLVES BUT RUN AWAY FROM MICE? I THINK?
NOBODY EVER MENTIONED ANGRY ORBS. MAYBE I'LL KICK IT.
LICK IT? NO WAY. I WANT TO BITE IT!
UM, IS ANYONE ELSE SUDDENLY HAVING A PROBLEM WITH THEIR CLOTHES? MY KNEEPADS ARE TRYING TO KILL ME!
ARE YOU SURE YOU AREN'T JUST HAVING A GROWTH SPURT?

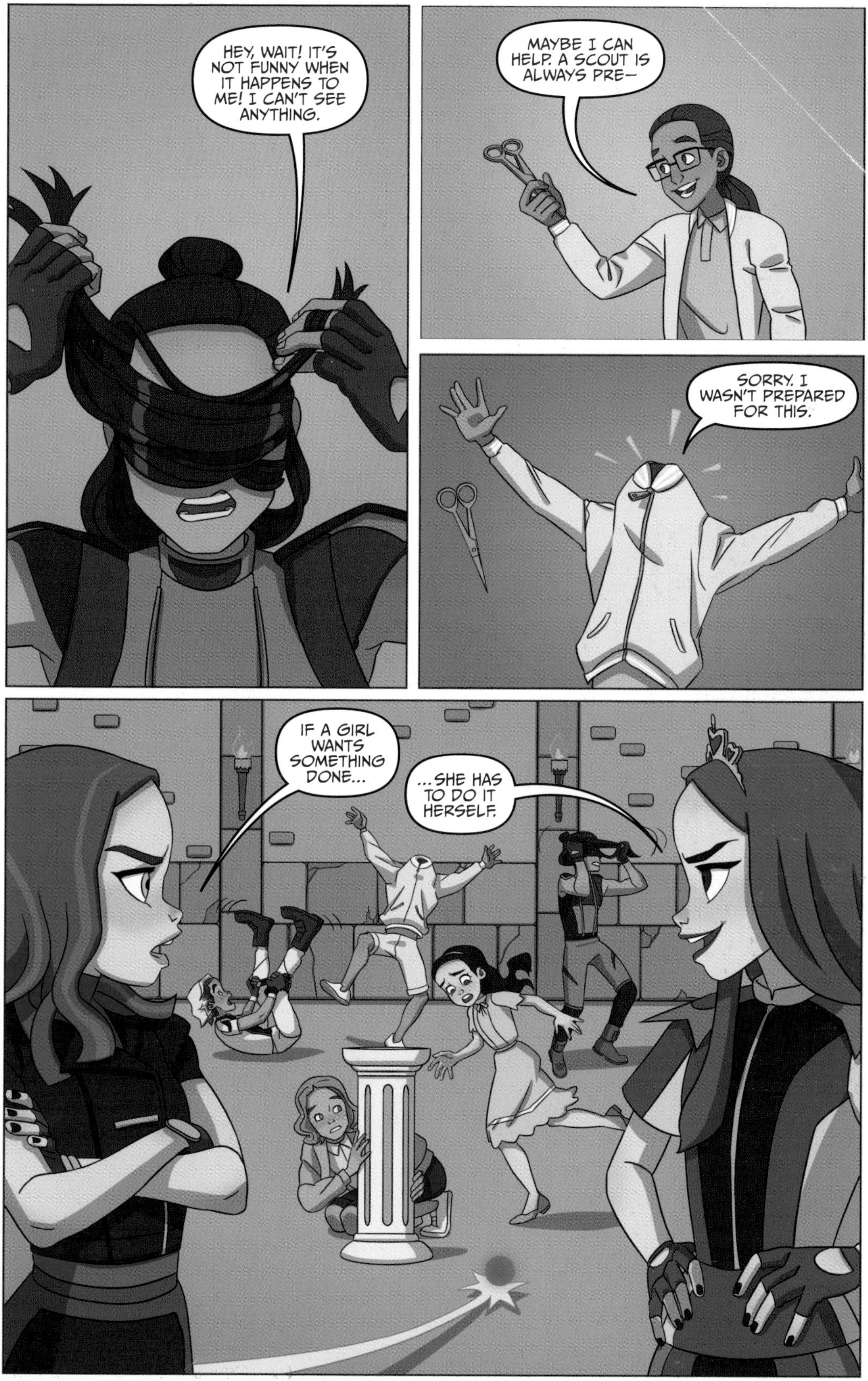
HEY, WAIT! IT'S NOT FUNNY WHEN IT HAPPENS TO ME! I CAN'T SEE ANYTHING.
MAYBE I CAN HELP. A SCOUT IS ALWAYS PRE—
SORRY. I WASN'T PREPARED FOR THIS.
IF A GIRL WANTS SOMETHING DONE...
...SHE HAS TO DO IT HERSELF.

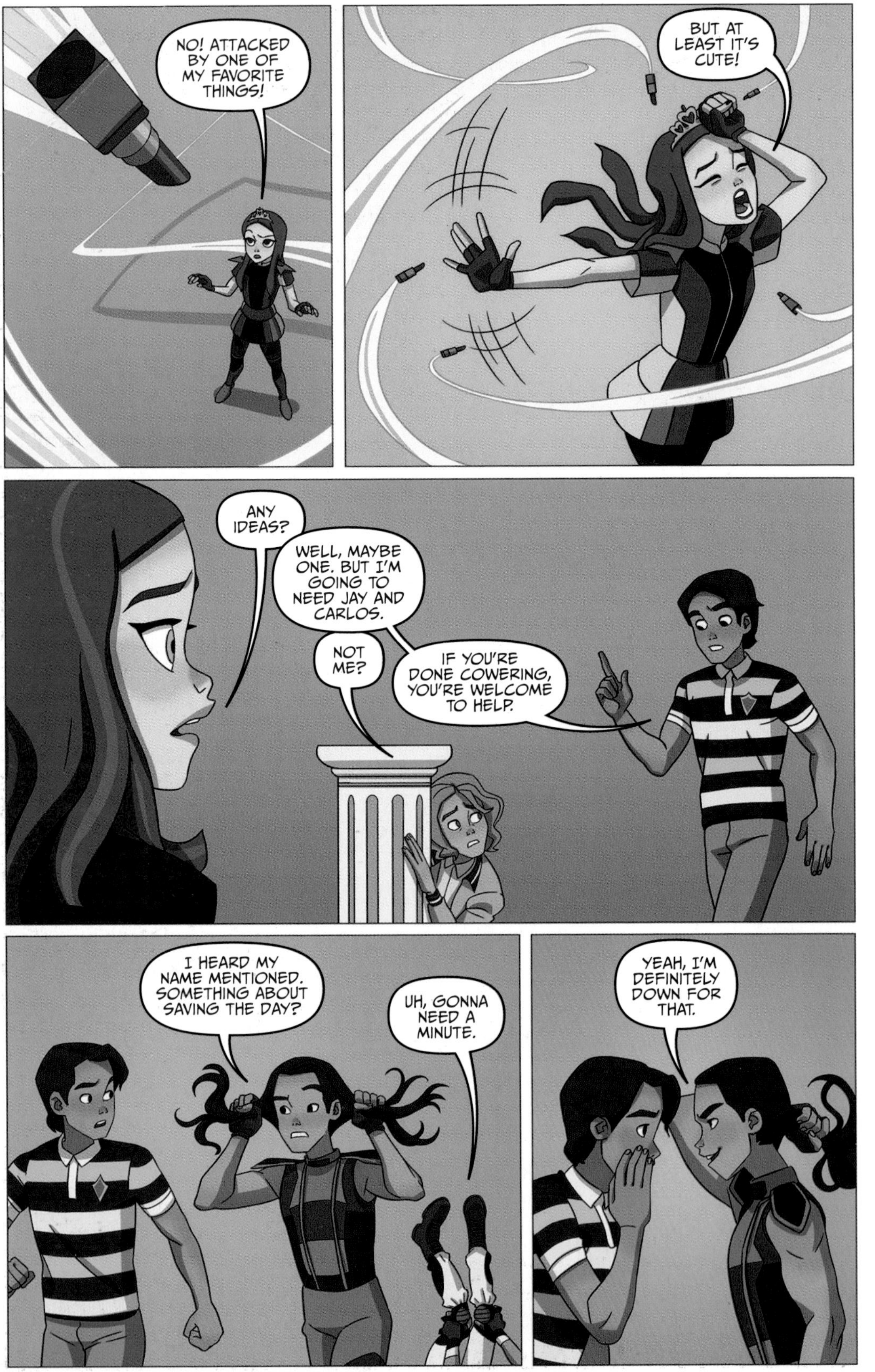
NO! ATTACKED BY ONE OF MY FAVORITE THINGS!
BUT AT LEAST IT'S CUTE!
ANY IDEAS?
WELL, MAYBE ONE. BUT I'M GOING TO NEED JAY AND CARLOS.
NOT ME?
IF YOU'RE DONE COWERING, YOU'RE WELCOME TO HELP.
I HEARD MY NAME MENTIONED. SOMETHING ABOUT SAVING THE DAY?
UH, GONNA NEED A MINUTE.
YEAH, I'M DEFINITELY DOWN FOR THAT.

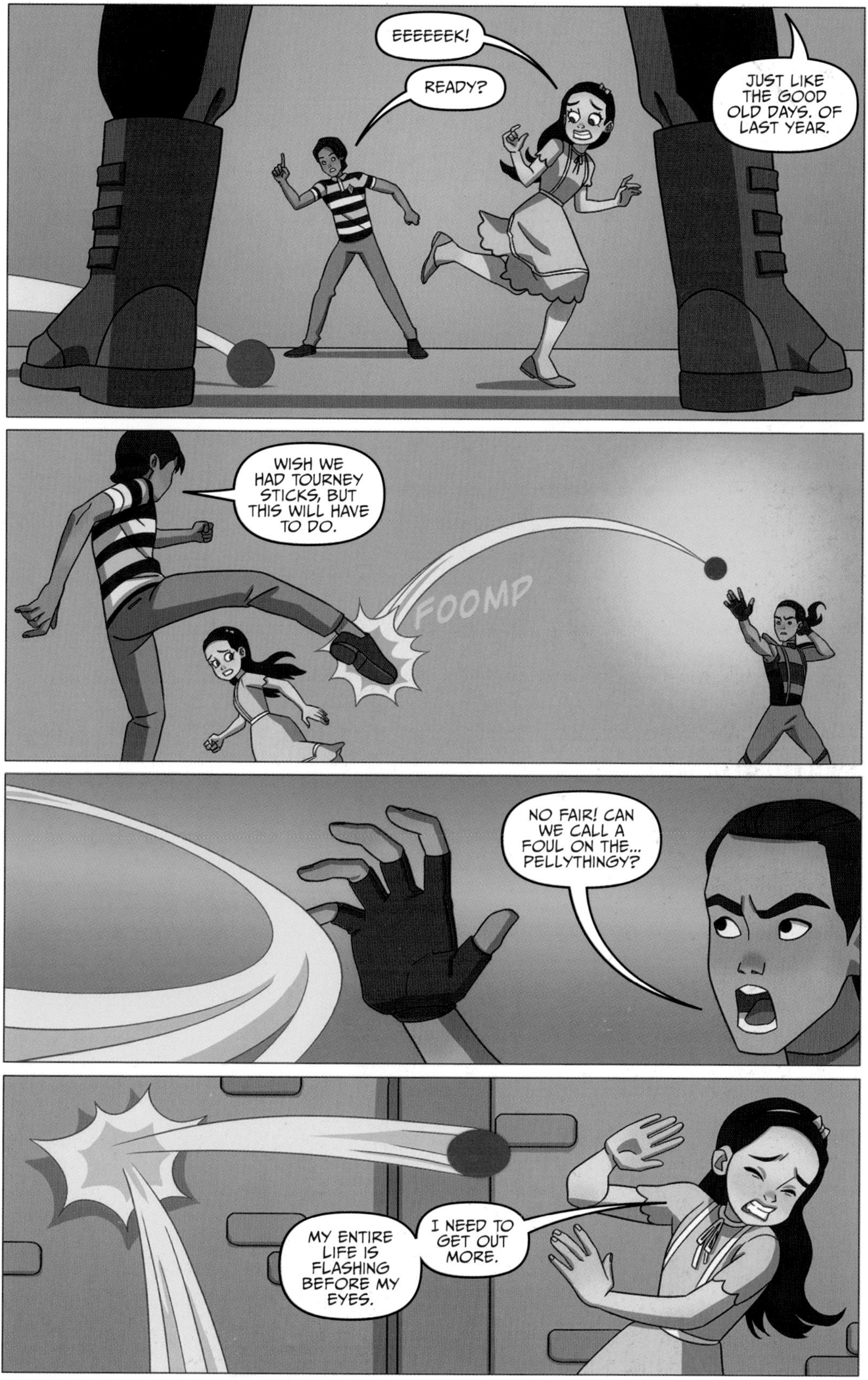
EEEEEEK!
READY?
JUST LIKE THE GOOD OLD DAYS. OF LAST YEAR.
WISH WE HAD TOURNEY STICKS, BUT THIS WILL HAVE TO DO.
FOOMP
NO FAIR! CAN WE CALL A FOUL ON THE... PELLYTHINGY?
MY ENTIRE LIFE IS FLASHING BEFORE MY EYES.
I NEED TO GET OUT MORE.

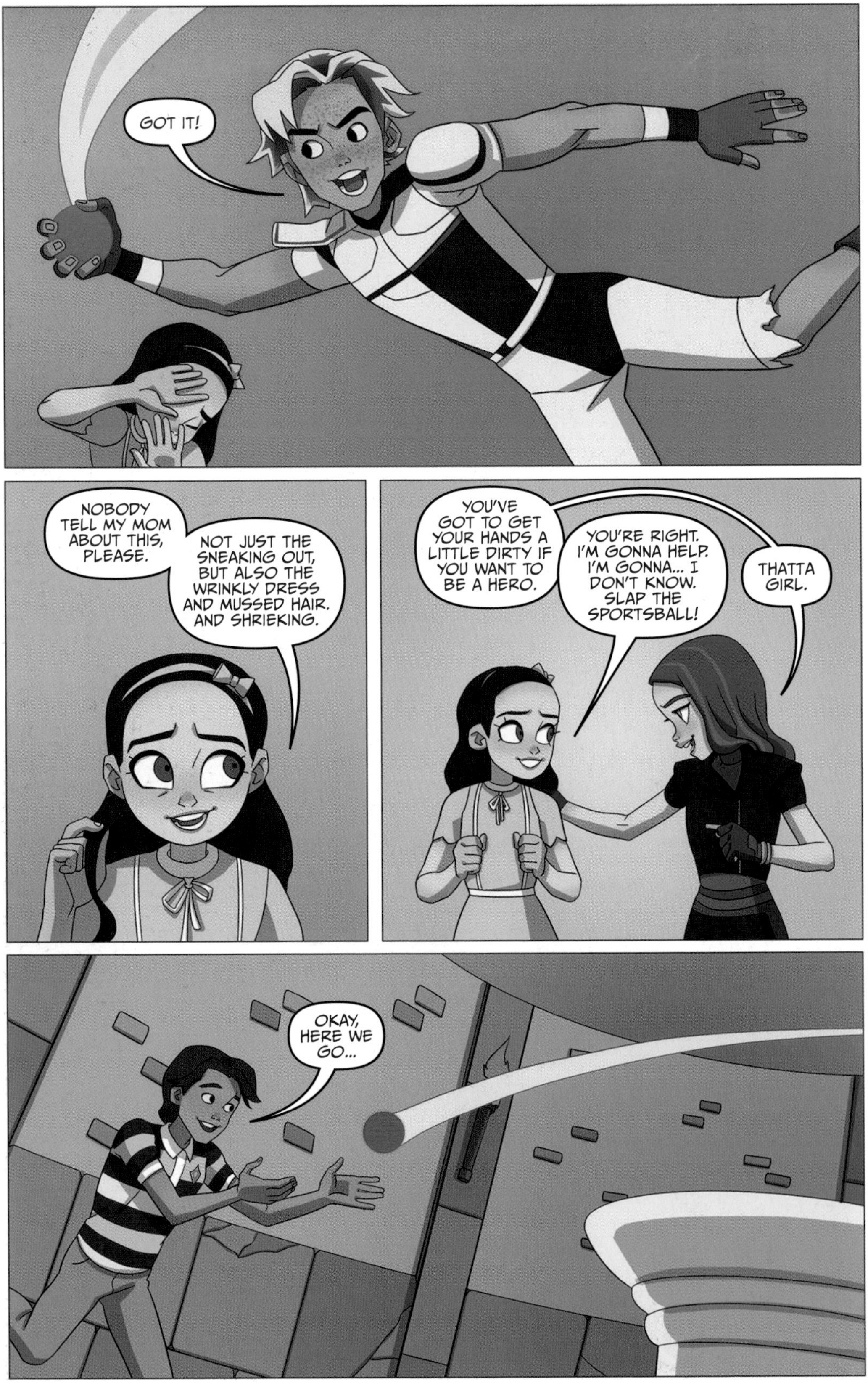
GOT IT!
NOBODY TELL MY MOM ABOUT THIS, PLEASE.
NOT JUST THE SNEAKING OUT, BUT ALSO THE WRINKLY DRESS AND MUSSED HAIR. AND SHRIEKING.
YOU'VE GOT TO GET YOUR HANDS A LITTLE DIRTY IF YOU WANT TO BE A HERO.
YOU'RE RIGHT. I'M GONNA HELP. I'M GONNA... I DON'T KNOW. SLAP THE SPORTSBALL!
THATTA GIRL.
OKAY, HERE WE GO...

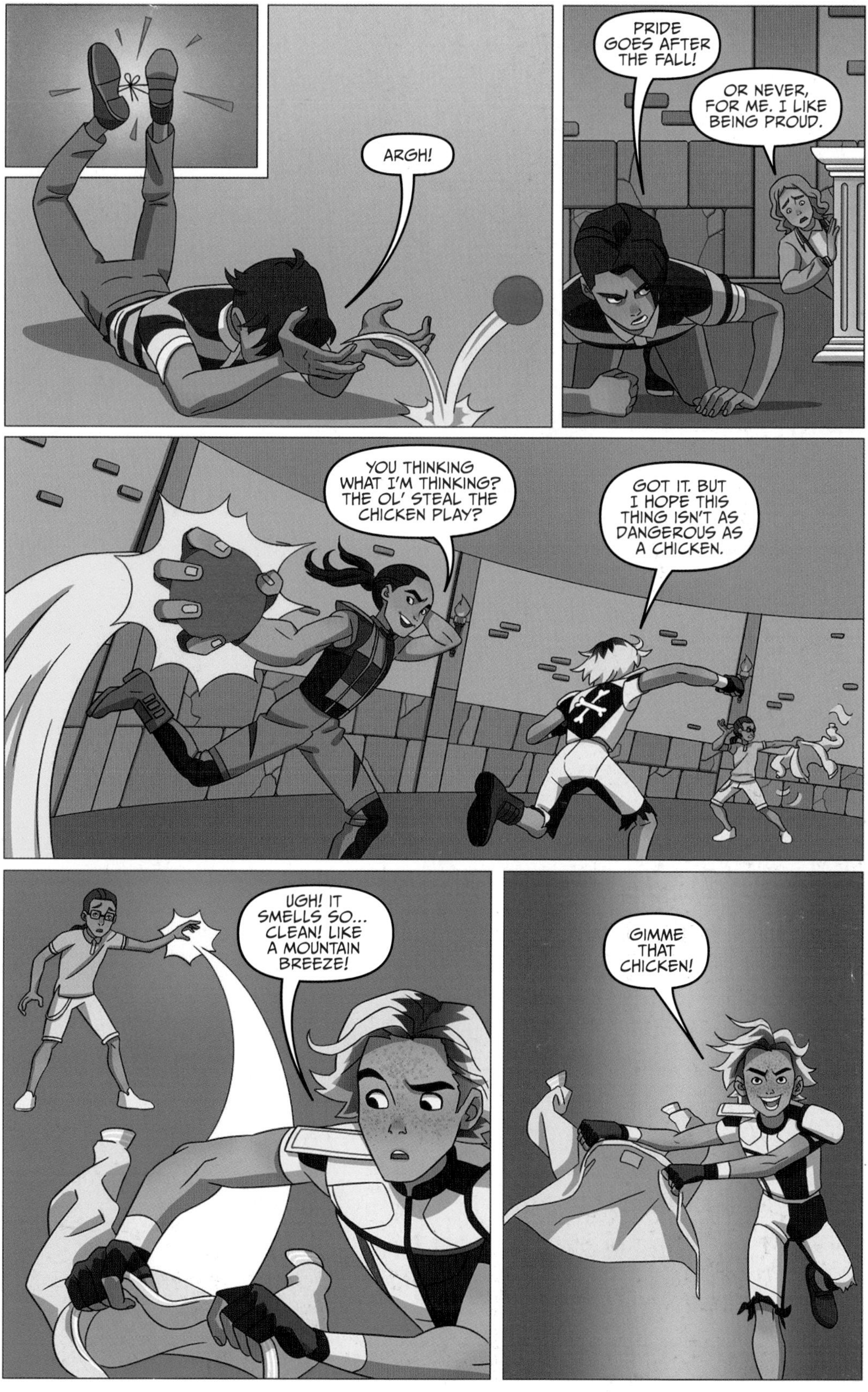
ARGH!
PRIDE GOES AFTER THE FALL!
OR NEVER, FOR ME. I LIKE BEING PROUD.
YOU THINKING WHAT I'M THINKING? THE OL' STEAL THE CHICKEN PLAY?
GOT IT. BUT I HOPE THIS THING ISN'T AS DANGEROUS AS A CHICKEN.
UGH! IT SMELLS SO... CLEAN! LIKE A MOUNTAIN BREEZE!
GIMME THAT CHICKEN!

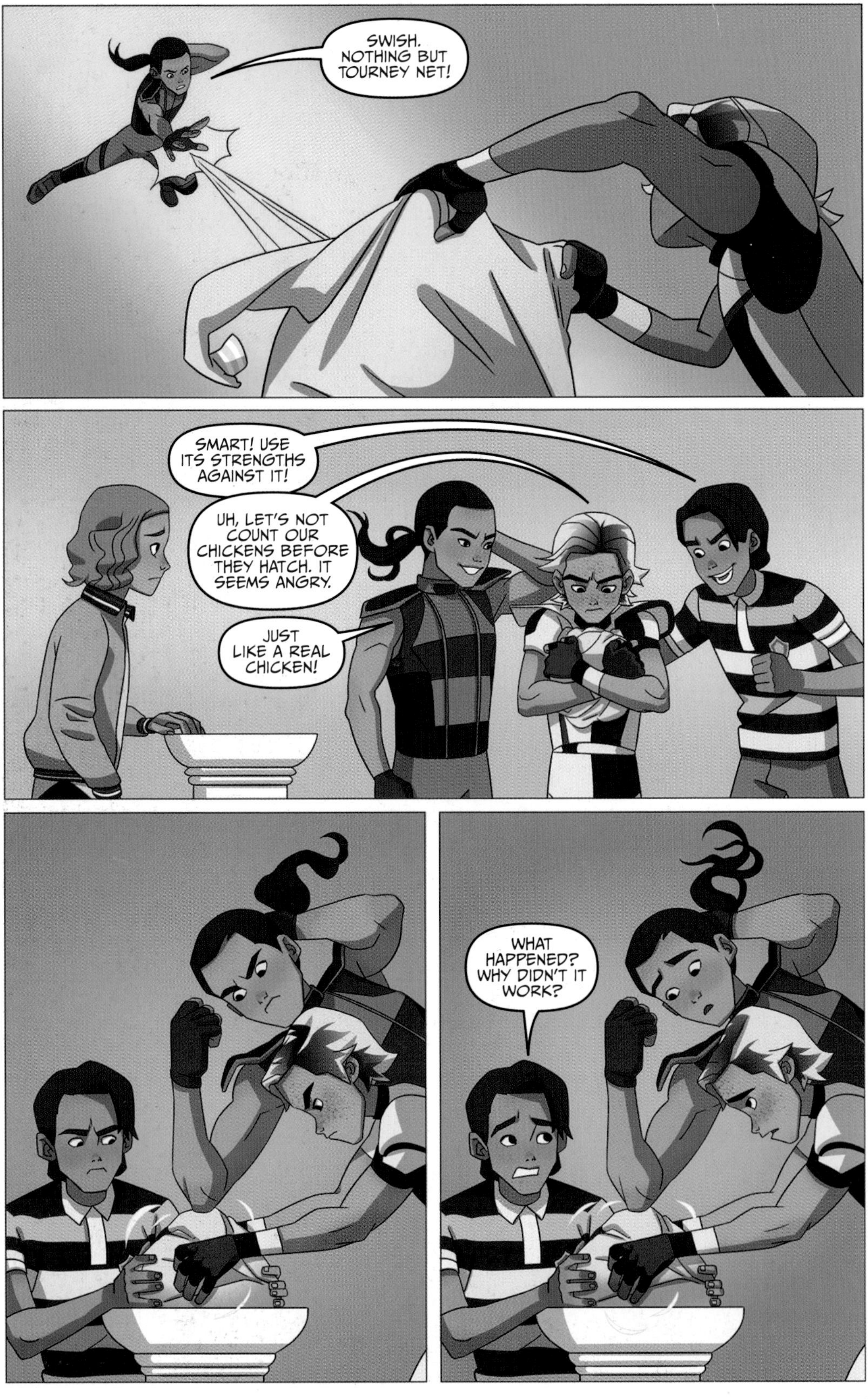
SWISH. NOTHING BUT TOURNEY NET!
SMART! USE ITS STRENGTHS AGAINST IT!
UH, LET'S NOT COUNT OUR CHICKENS BEFORE THEY HATCH. IT SEEMS ANGRY.
JUST LIKE A REAL CHICKEN!
WHAT HAPPENED? WHY DIDN'T IT WORK?

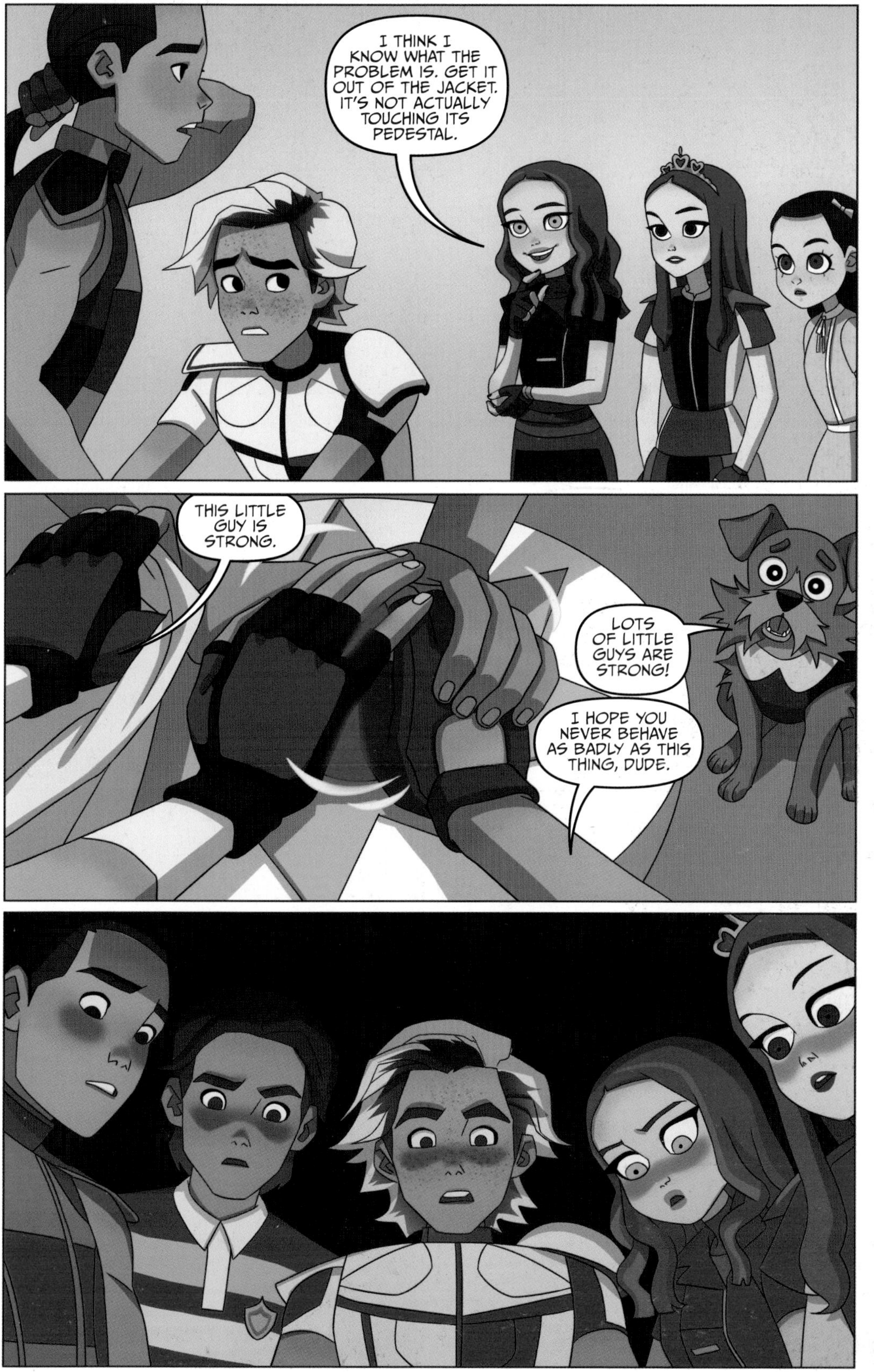
I THINK I KNOW WHAT THE PROBLEM IS. GET IT OUT OF THE JACKET. IT'S NOT ACTUALLY TOUCHING ITS PEDESTAL.
THIS LITTLE GUY IS STRONG.
LOTS OF LITTLE GUYS ARE STRONG!
I HOPE YOU NEVER BEHAVE AS BADLY AS THIS THING, DUDE.

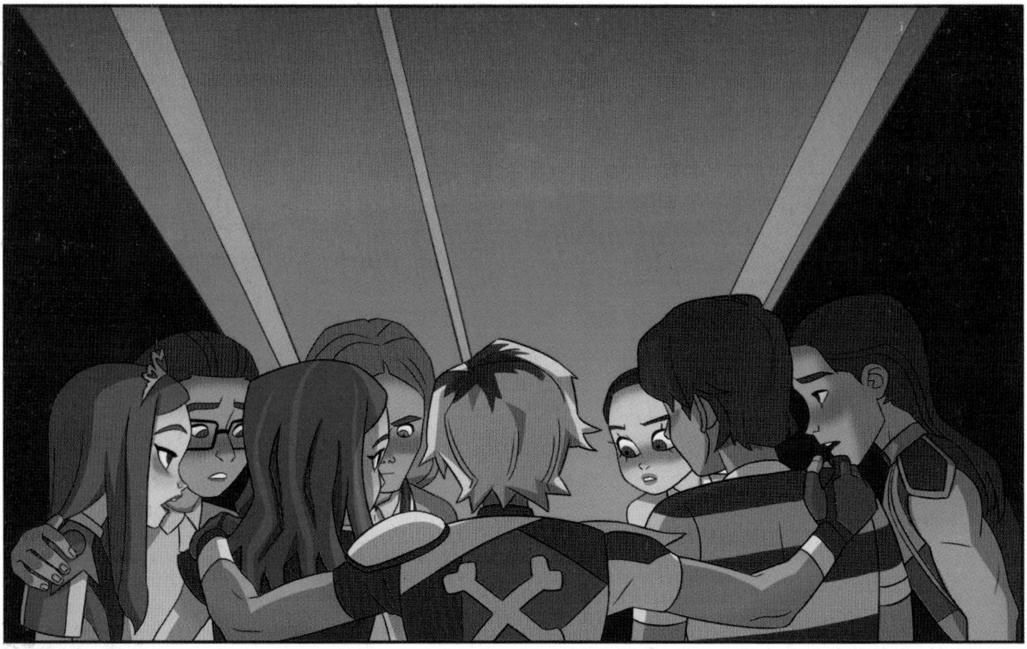

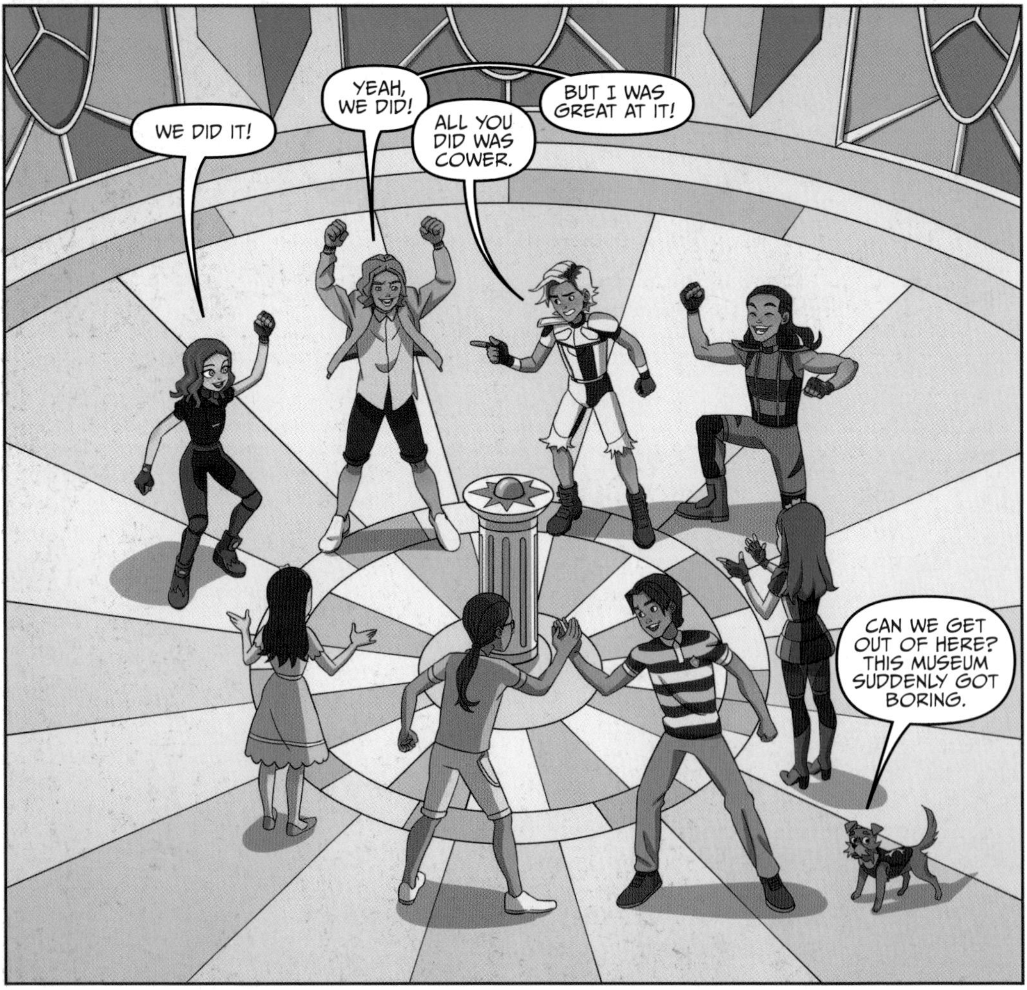
WE DID IT!
YEAH, WE DID!
ALL YOU DID WAS COWER.
BUT I WAS GREAT AT IT!
CAN WE GET OUT OF HERE? THIS MUSEUM SUDDENLY GOT BORING.

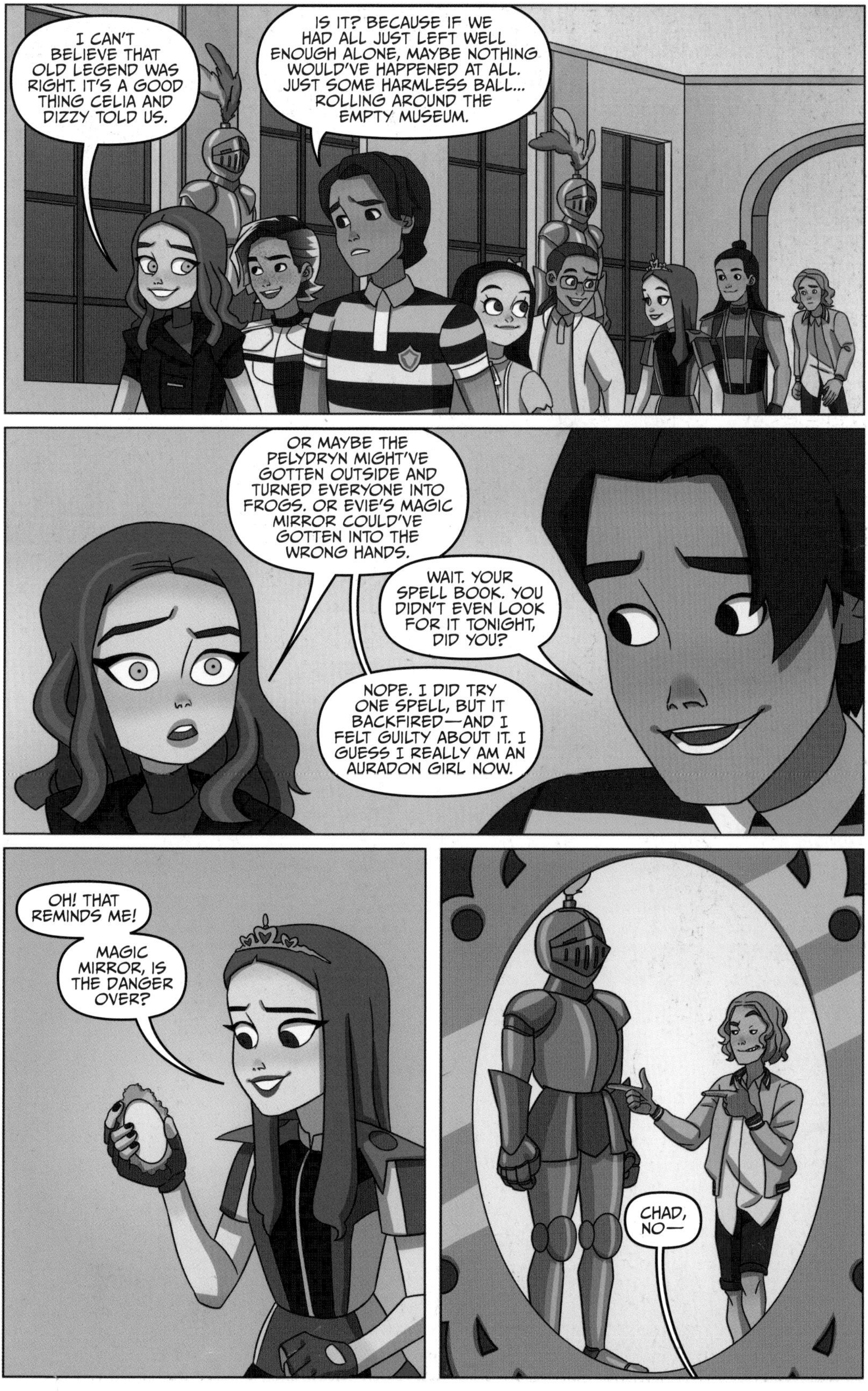
I CAN'T BELIEVE THAT OLD LEGEND WAS RIGHT. IT'S A GOOD THING CELIA AND DIZZY TOLD US.
IS IT? BECAUSE IF WE HAD ALL JUST LEFT WELL ENOUGH ALONE, MAYBE NOTHING WOULD'VE HAPPENED AT ALL. JUST SOME HARMLESS BALL... ROLLING AROUND THE EMPTY MUSEUM.
OR MAYBE THE PELYDRYN MIGHT'VE GOTTEN OUTSIDE AND TURNED EVERYONE INTO FROGS. OR EVIE'S MAGIC MIRROR COULD'VE GOTTEN INTO THE WRONG HANDS.
WAIT. YOUR SPELL BOOK. YOU DIDN'T EVEN LOOK FOR IT TONIGHT, DID YOU?
NOPE. I DID TRY ONE SPELL, BUT IT BACKFIRED—AND I FELT GUILTY ABOUT IT. I GUESS I REALLY AM AN AURADON GIRL NOW.
OH! THAT REMINDS ME!
MAGIC MIRROR, IS THE DANGER OVER?
CHAD, NO—

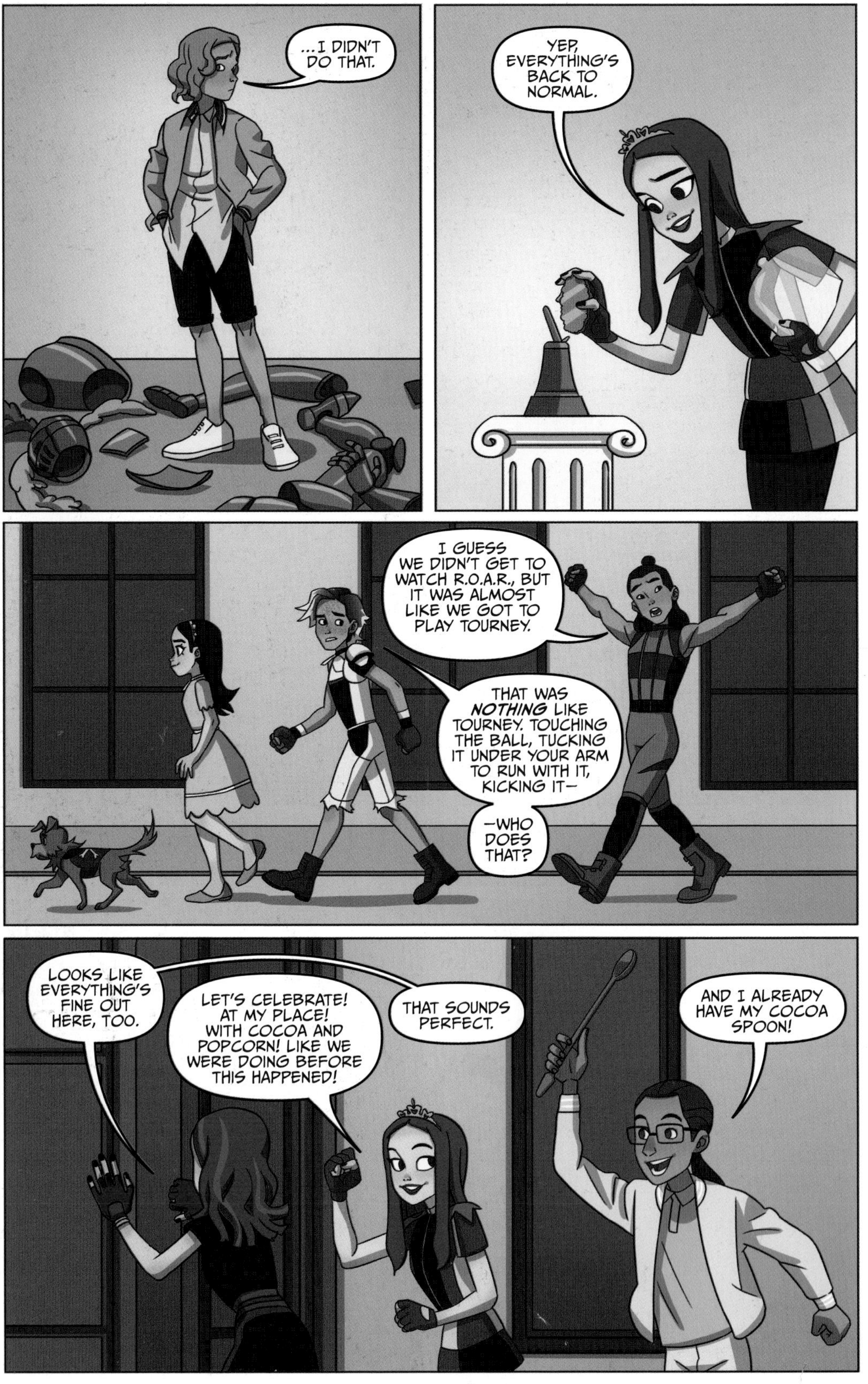
...I DIDN'T DO THAT.
YEP, EVERYTHING'S BACK TO NORMAL.
I GUESS WE DIDN'T GET TO WATCH R.O.A.R., BUT IT WAS ALMOST LIKE WE GOT TO PLAY TOURNEY.
THAT WAS *NOTHING* LIKE TOURNEY. TOUCHING THE BALL, TUCKING IT UNDER YOUR ARM TO RUN WITH IT, KICKING IT—
—WHO DOES THAT?
LOOKS LIKE EVERYTHING'S FINE OUT HERE, TOO.
LET'S CELEBRATE! AT MY PLACE! WITH COCOA AND POPCORN! LIKE WE WERE DOING BEFORE THIS HAPPENED!
THAT SOUNDS PERFECT.
AND I ALREADY HAVE MY COCOA SPOON!

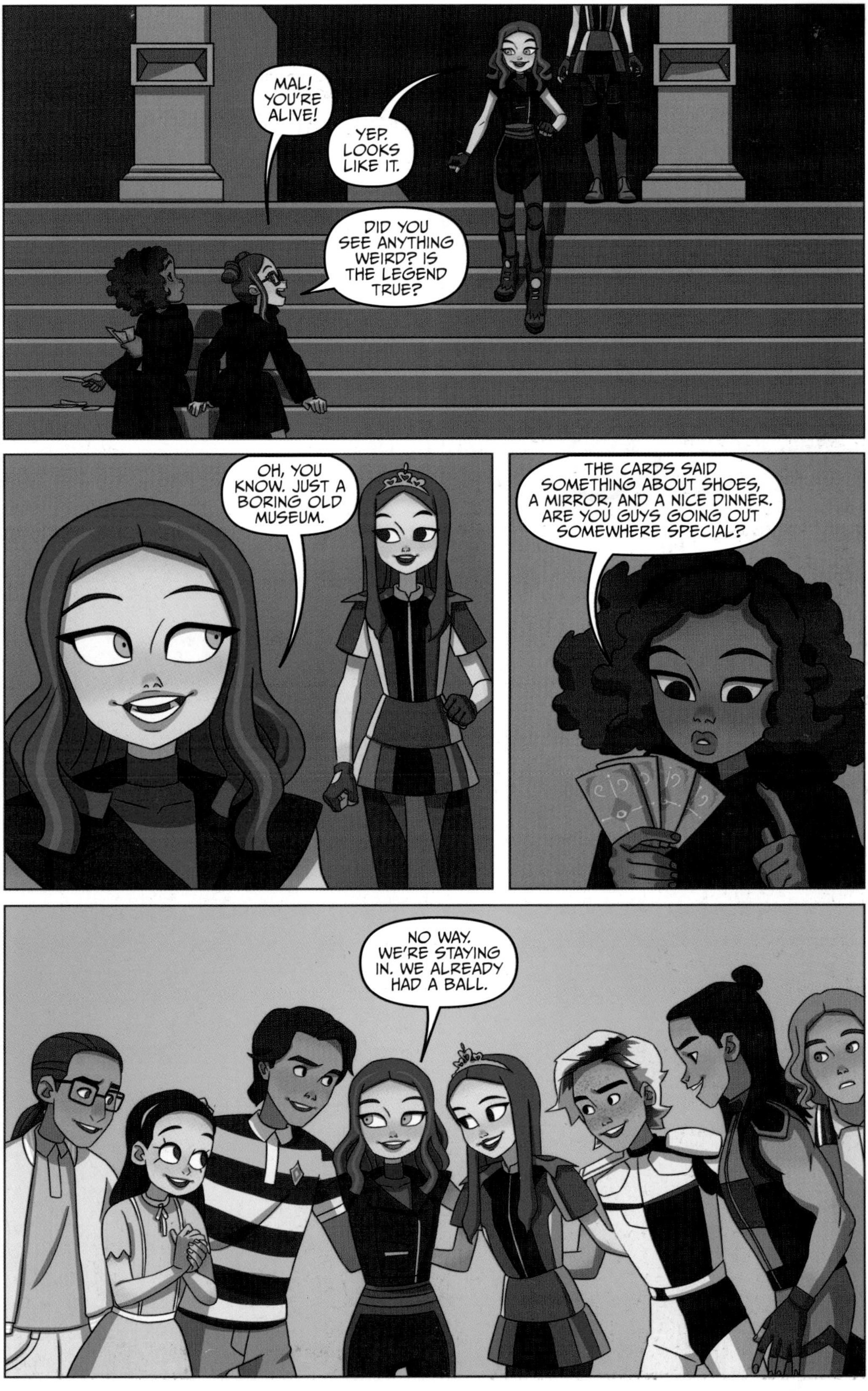
MAL! YOU'RE ALIVE!
YEP. LOOKS LIKE IT.
DID YOU SEE ANYTHING WEIRD? IS THE LEGEND TRUE?
OH, YOU KNOW. JUST A BORING OLD MUSEUM.
THE CARDS SAID SOMETHING ABOUT SHOES, A MIRROR, AND A NICE DINNER. ARE YOU GUYS GOING OUT SOMEWHERE SPECIAL?
NO WAY. WE'RE STAYING IN. WE ALREADY HAD A BALL.

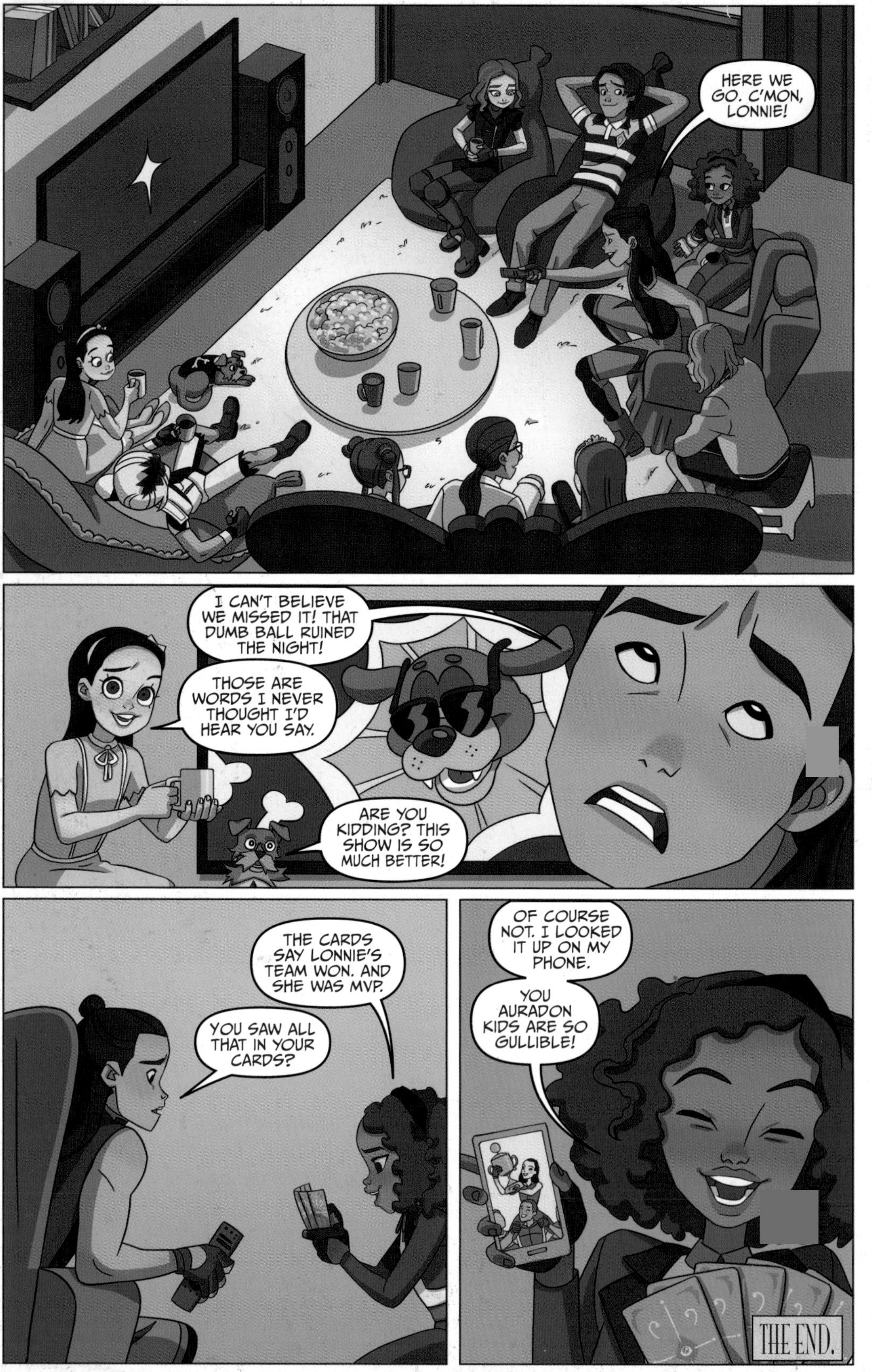
HERE WE GO. C'MON, LONNIE!
I CAN'T BELIEVE WE MISSED IT! THAT DUMB BALL RUINED THE NIGHT!
THOSE ARE WORDS I NEVER THOUGHT I'D HEAR YOU SAY.
ARE YOU KIDDING? THIS SHOW IS SO MUCH BETTER!
THE CARDS SAY LONNIE'S TEAM WON. AND SHE WAS MVP.
YOU SAW ALL THAT IN YOUR CARDS?
OF COURSE NOT. I LOOKED IT UP ON MY PHONE.
YOU AURADON KIDS ARE SO GULLIBLE!
THE END.

PHOTO GALLERY

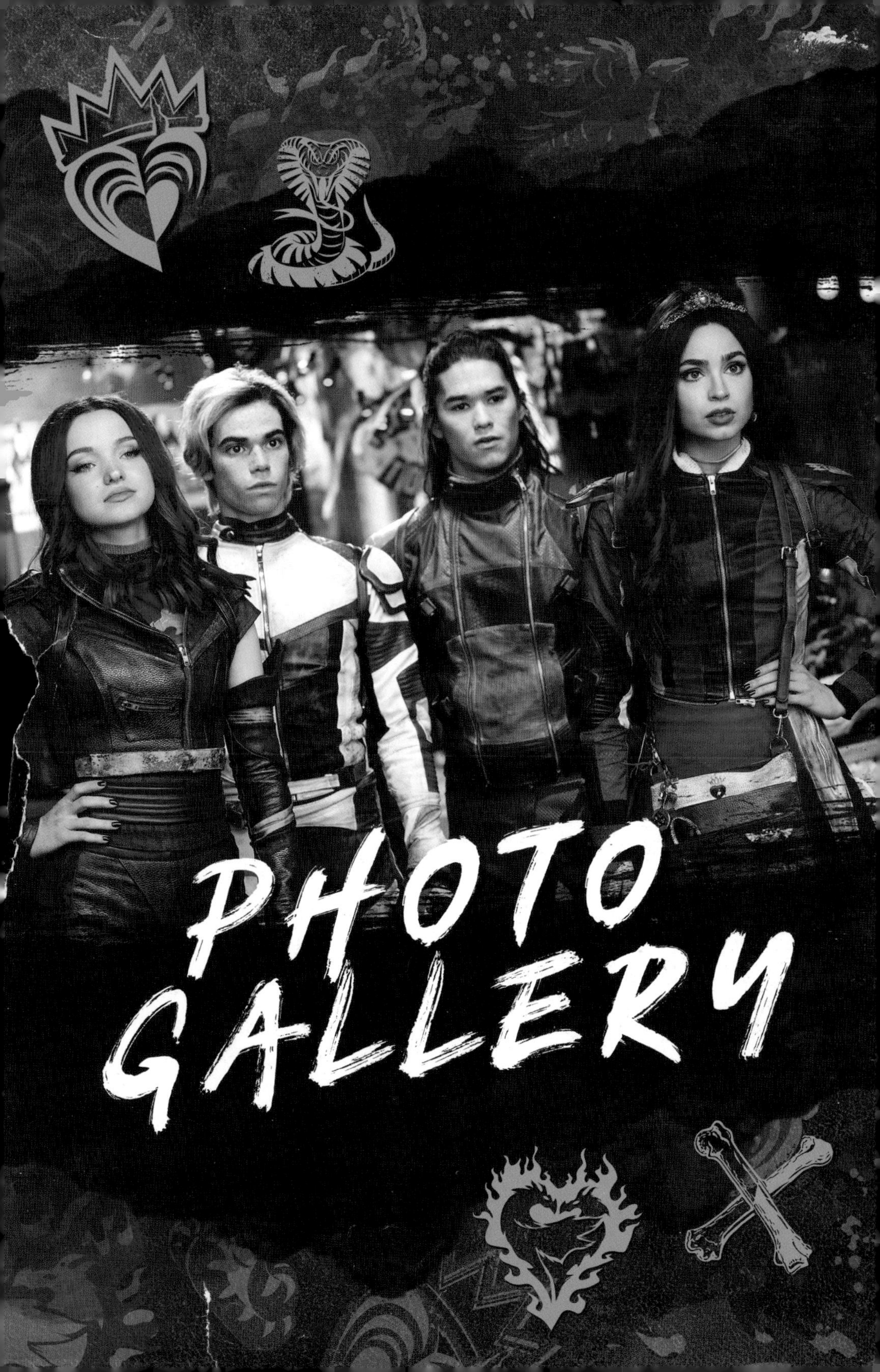

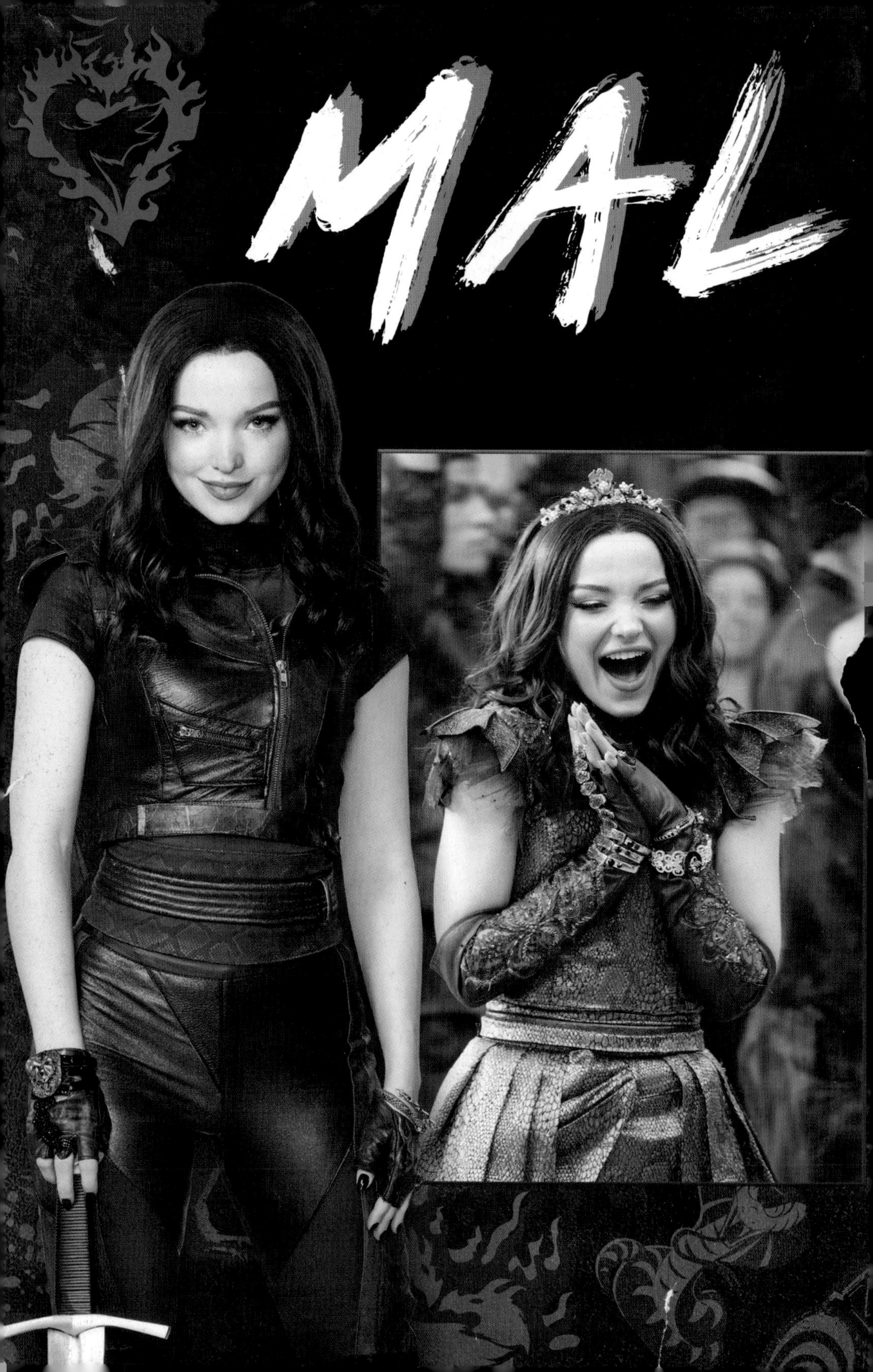
MAL

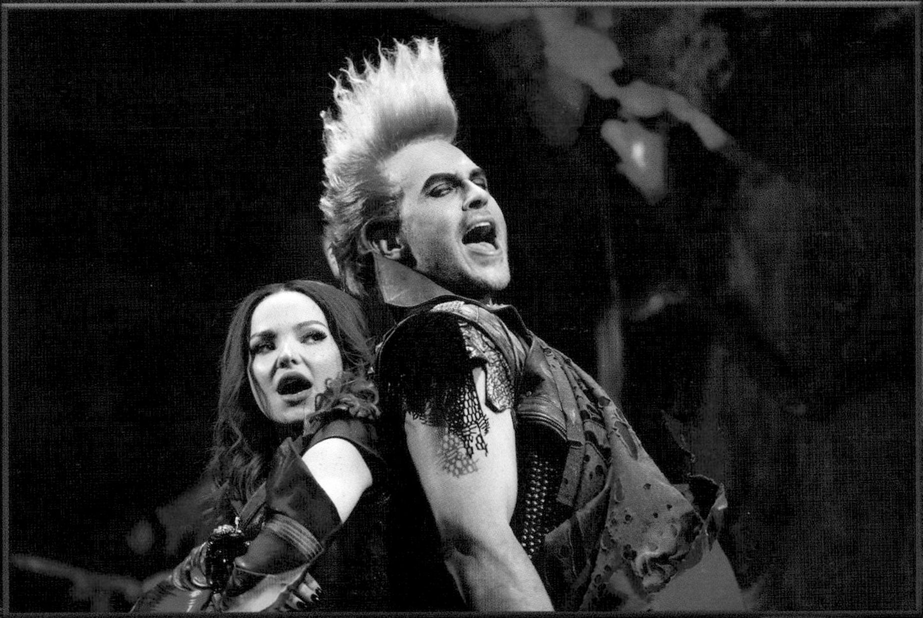

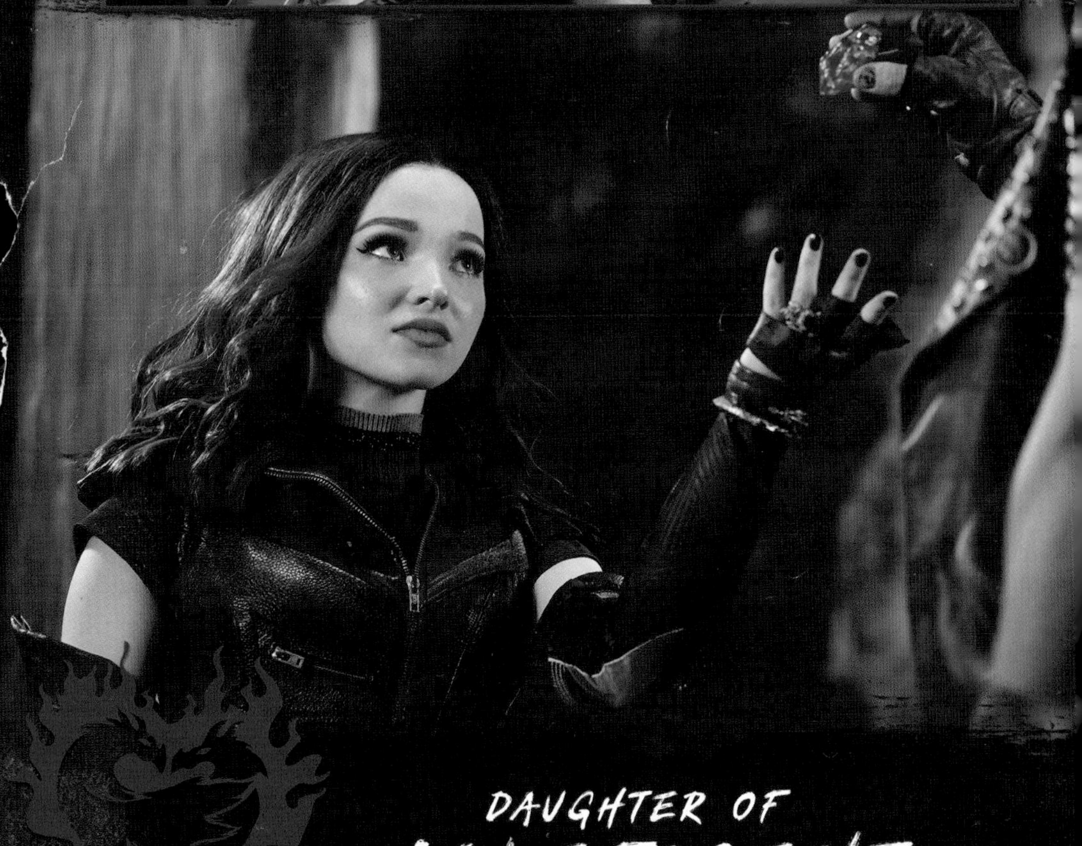

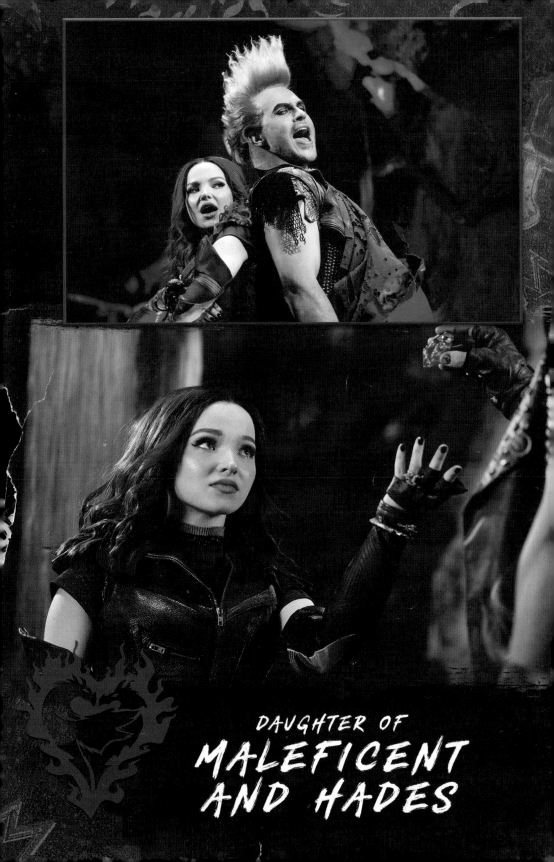

DAUGHTER OF

MALEFICENT AND HADES

DAUGHTER OF
EVIL
QUEEN

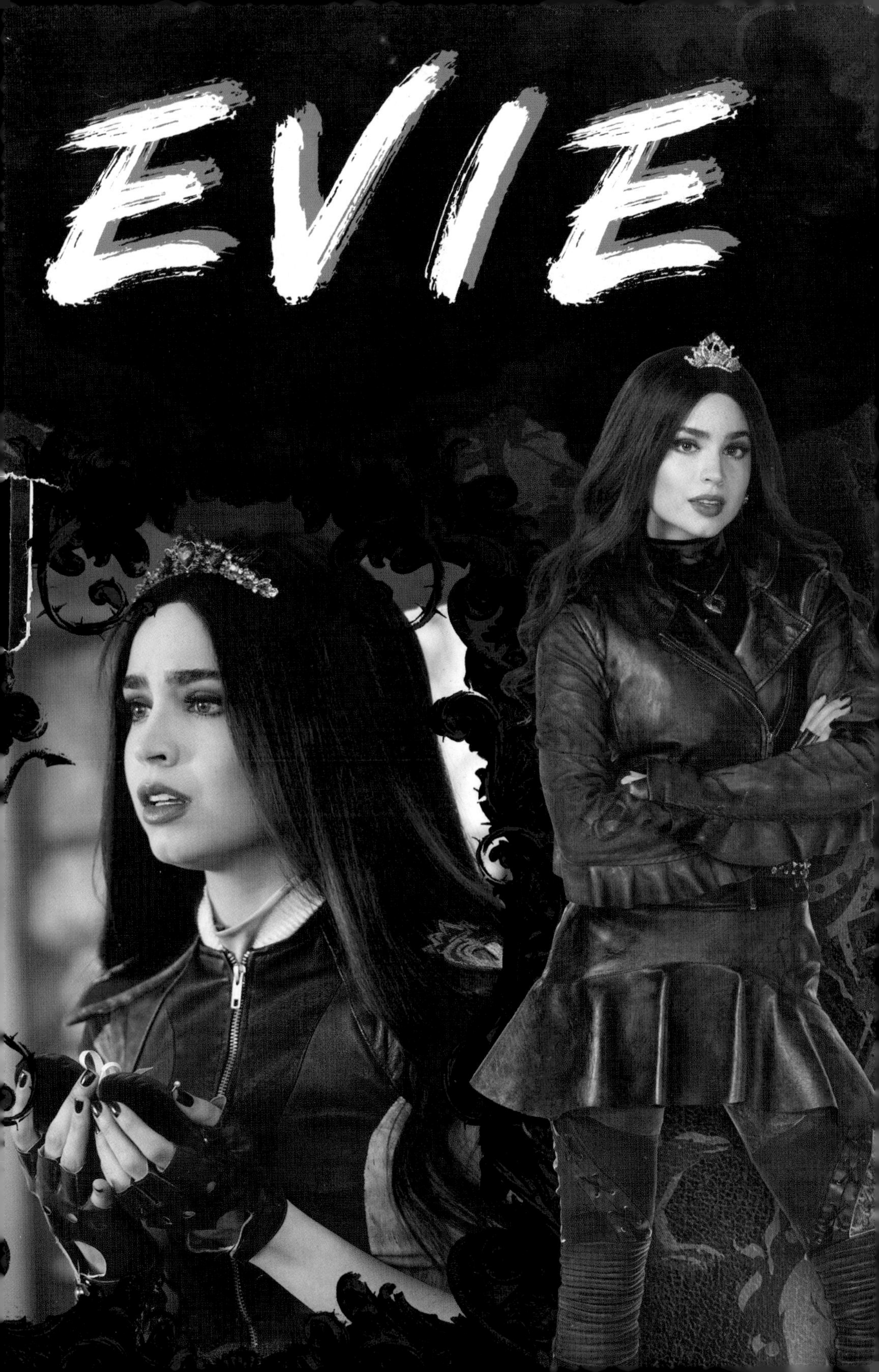
EVIE

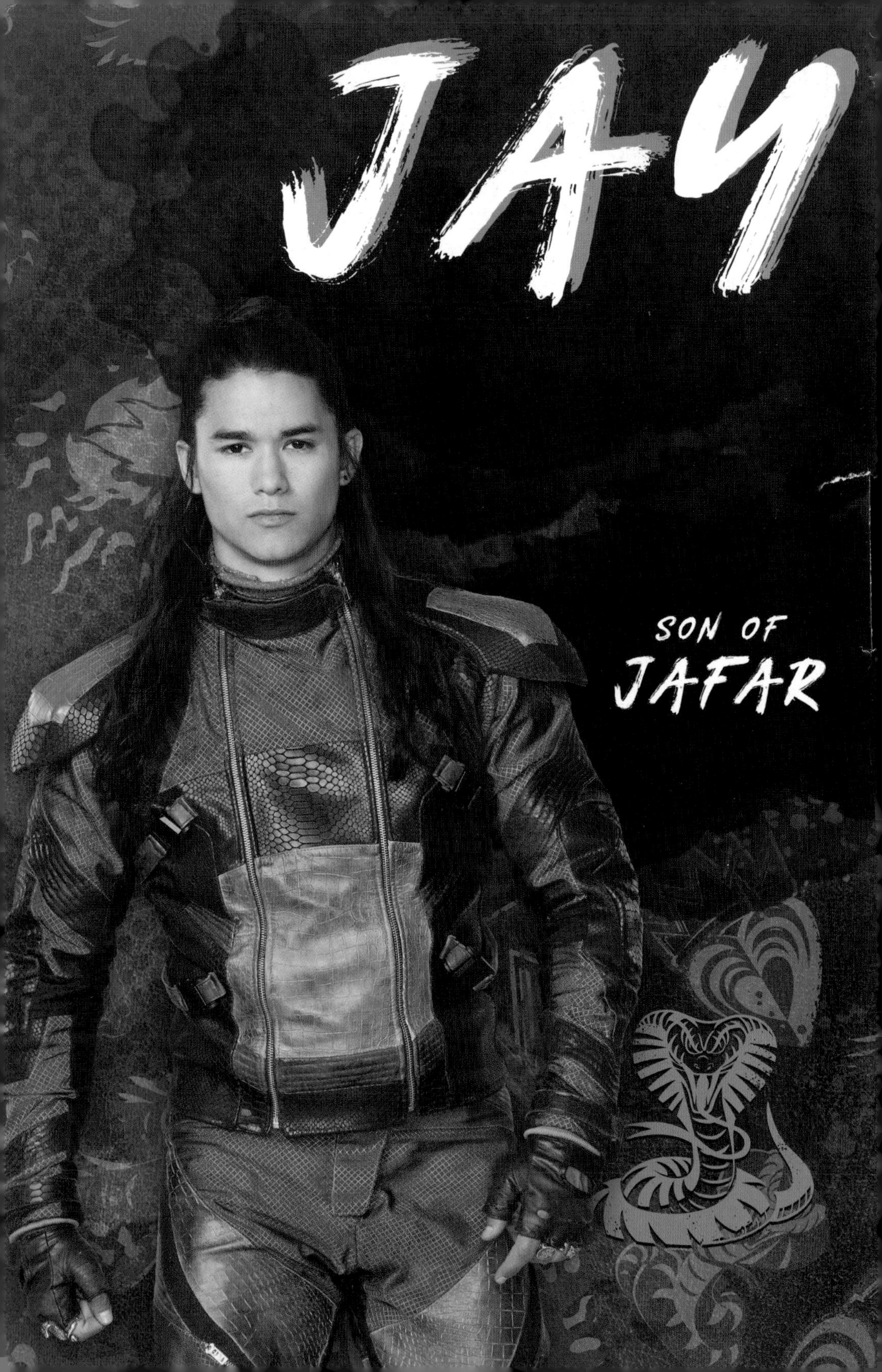
JAY
SON OF
JAFAR

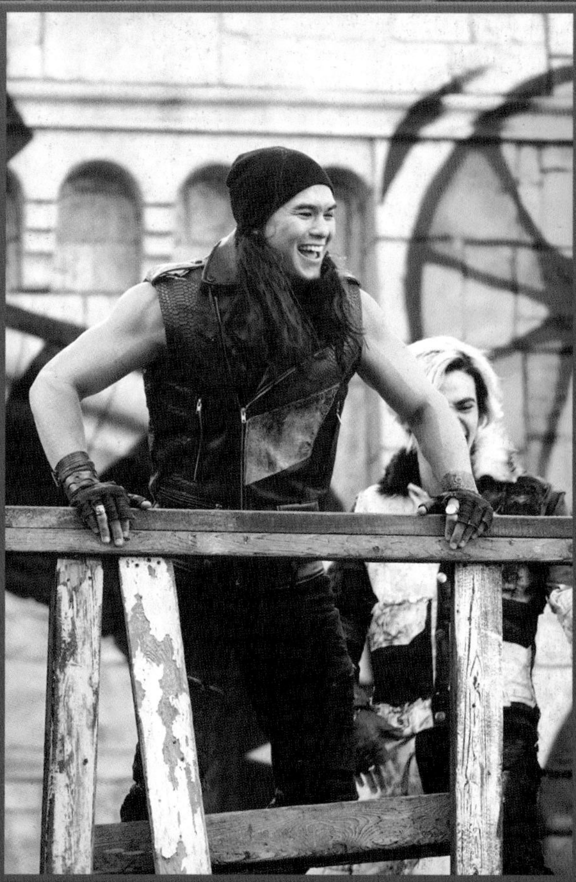

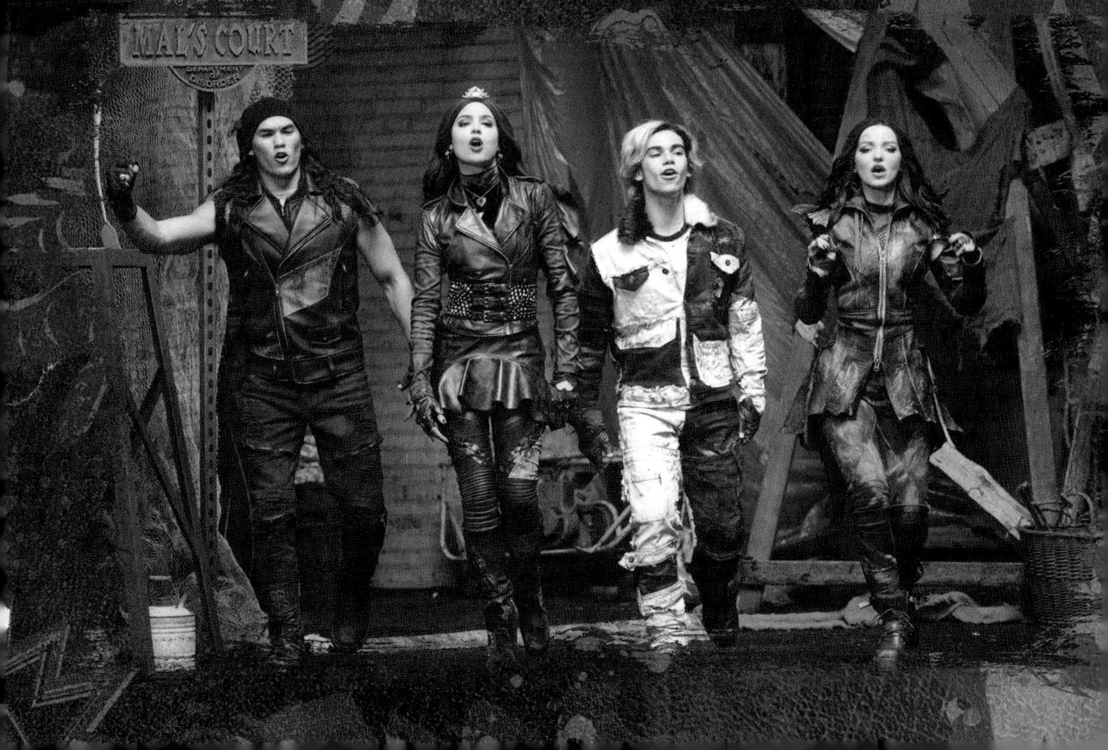
MAL'S COURT
DEPARTMENT OF DISORDER

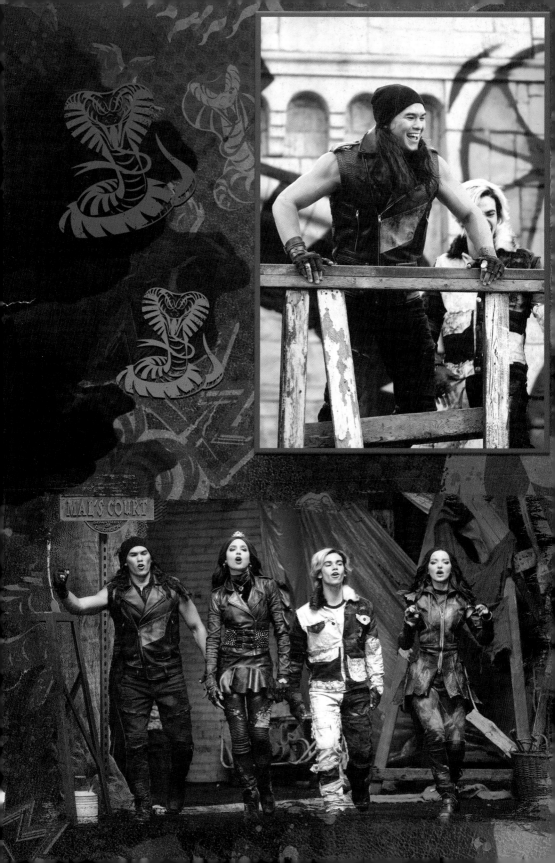

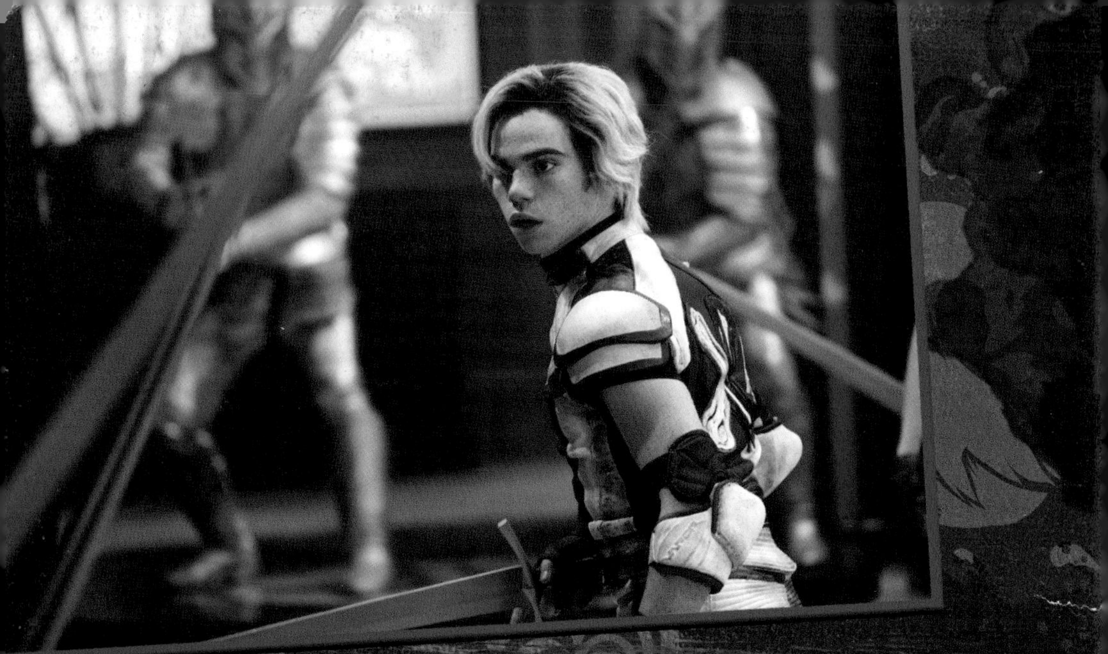

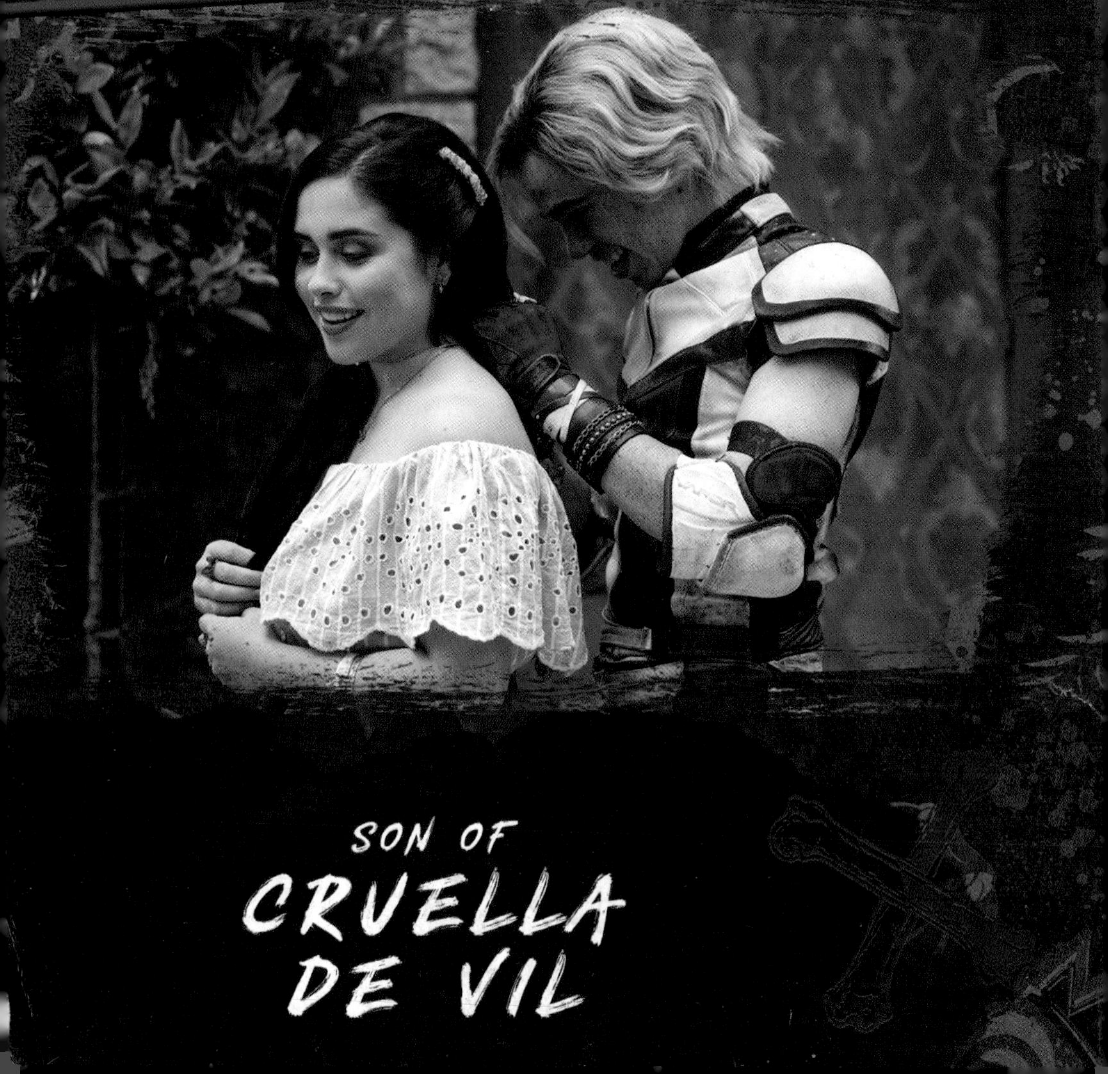

SON OF

CRUELLA DE VIL

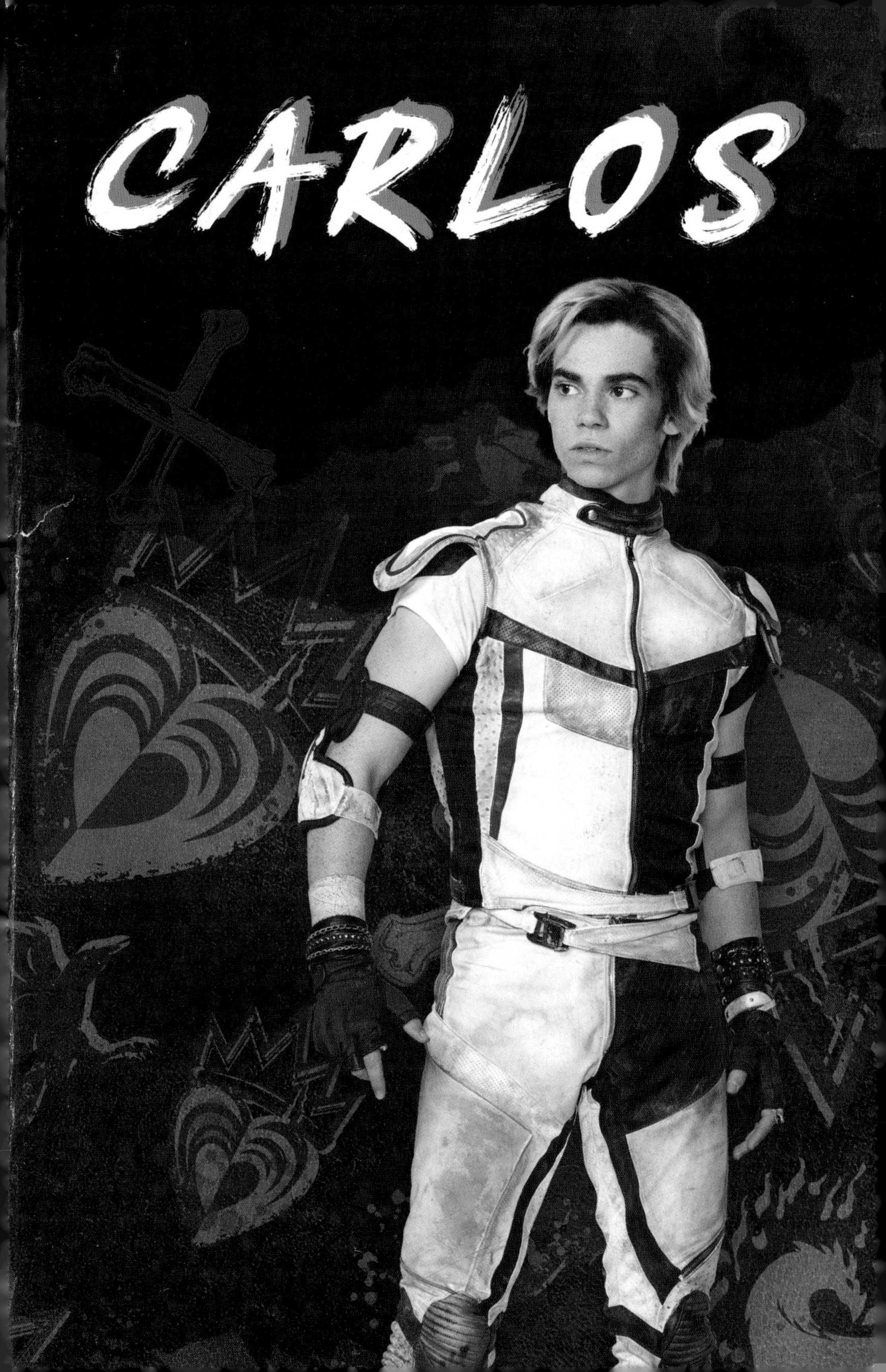
CARLOS

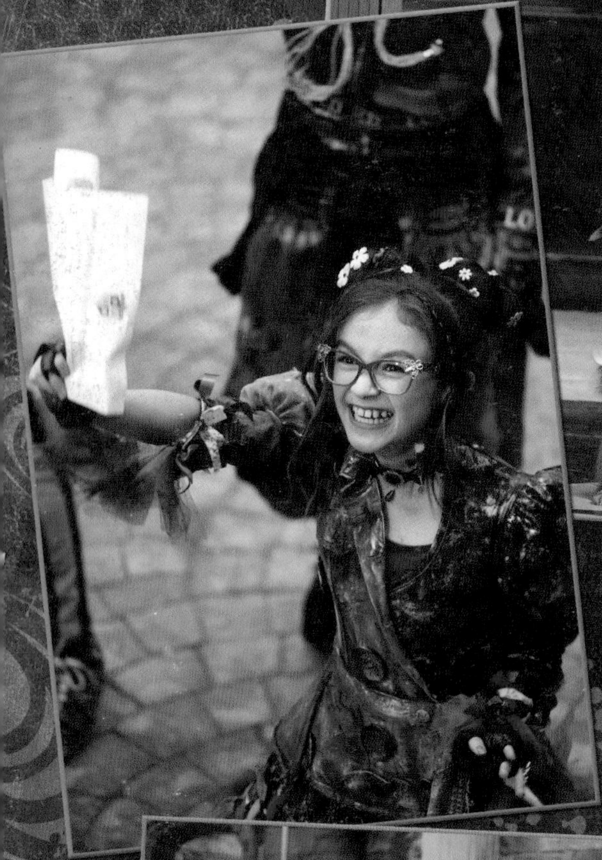

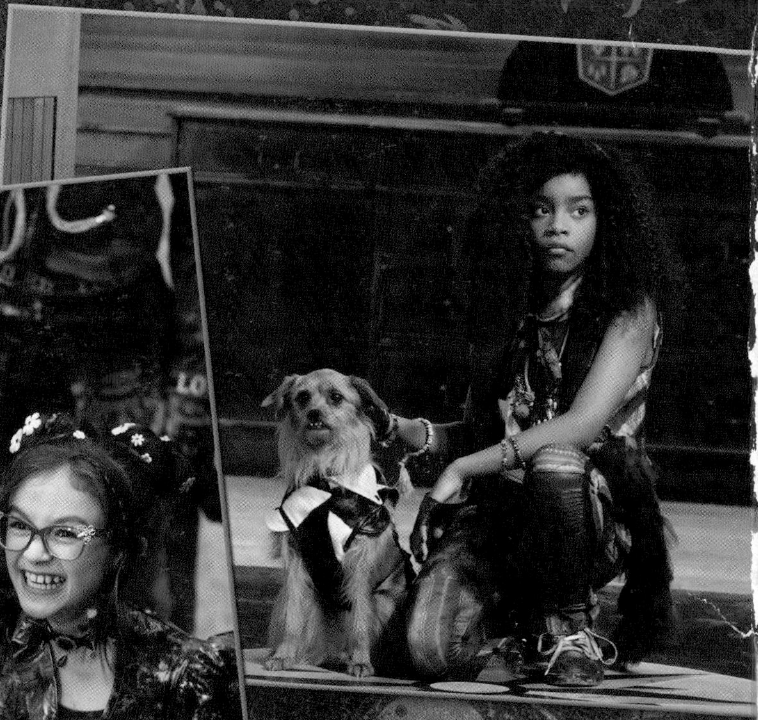

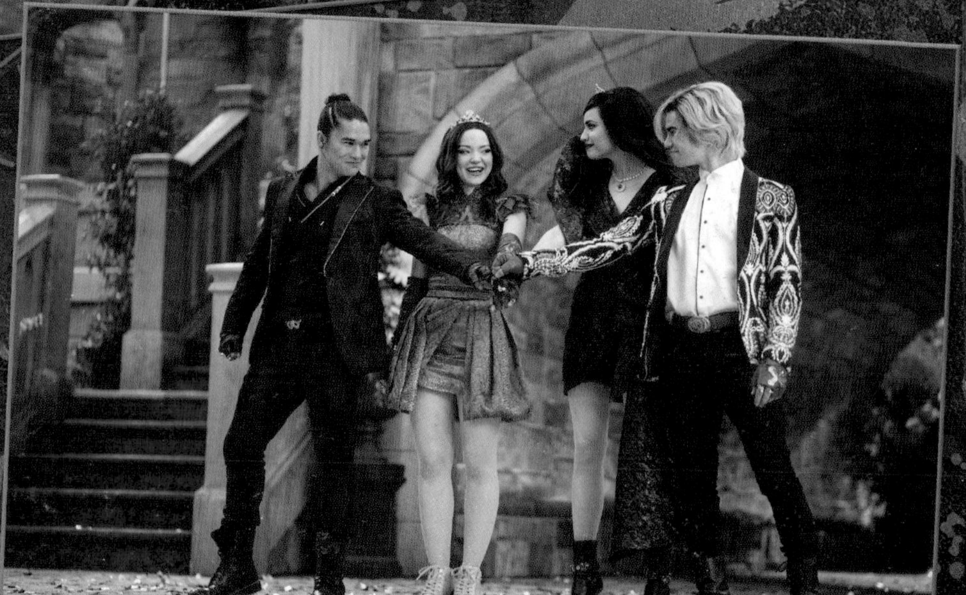

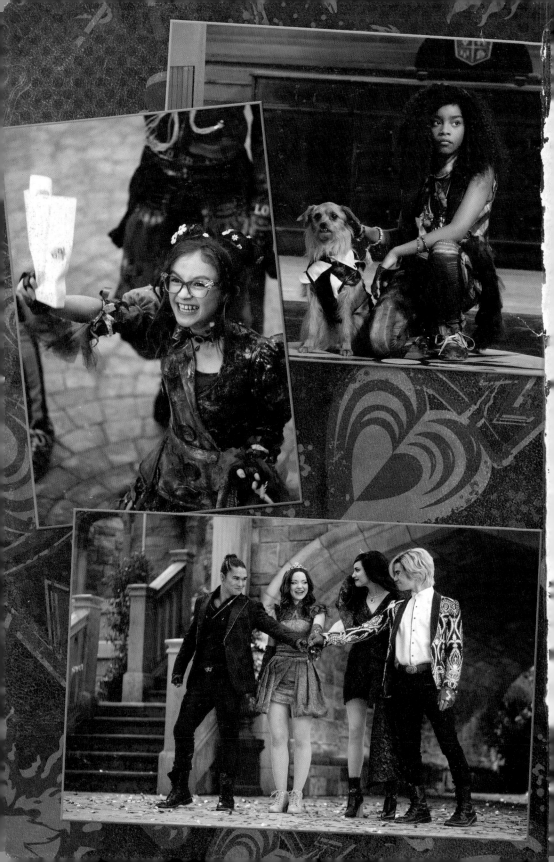